CHRIS CRUTCHER
Whale Talk

GREENWILLOW BOOKS
An Imprint of HarperCollins*Publishers*

Library of Congress Cataloging-in-Publication Data

Crutcher, Chris.
Whale talk / by Chris Crutcher
p.   cm.
"Greenwillow Books."
Summary: Intellectually and athletically gifted, T. J., a multiracial,
adopted teenager, shuns organized sports and the gung-ho athletes at his
high school until he agrees to form a swimming team and recruits some
of the school's less popular students.
ISBN 0-688-18019-1 (trade)   ISBN 0-06-029369-1 (lib. bdg.)
[1. Sports—Fiction.   2. Swimming—Fiction.   3. High schools—Fiction.
4. Schools—Fiction.   5. Racially mixed people—Fiction.
6. Adoption—Fiction.]   I. Title.
PZ7.C89 Wh 2001   [Fic]—dc21   00-059292

10   9   8

First Edition

For Ben Dodge
(1982–1997)

1

In the end, write it down. Back up and find the story. Mr. Simet, my English and journalism teacher says the best way to write a story, be it fact or fiction, is to believe aliens will find it someday and make a movie, and you don't want them making *Ishtar*. The trick is to dig out the people and events that connect, and connect them. No need to worry about who's wearing Nike and who's wearing Reebok, or anybody's hat size or percentage of body fat. Like Jack Webb on the *Dragnet* series on Nick at Nite says, "Just the facts, ma'am. Just the facts."

The facts. I'm black. And Japanese. And white. Politically correct would be African-American, Japanese-American and what? Northern European–American? God, by the time I wrote all that on a job application the position would be filled. Besides, I've never been to Africa, never been to Japan, and don't even know which countries make up Northern Europe. Plus, I know next to nothing about the individuals who contributed all that exotic DNA, so it's hard to carve out a cultural identity in my mind. So: Mixed. Blended. Pureed. Potpourri.

Adopted.

Big deal; so was Superman.

And like Superman, I was adopted by great people. The woman I call Mom—who *is* Mom—Abby Jones, was in the

1

hospital following her fourth miscarriage (and final attempt at the miracle of birth) where she met my biological mother, Glenda, right after my presumed bio-dad, Stephan, had assisted in my natural childbirth only to come eyeball-to-eyeball with the aforementioned UNICEF poster boy. A second-generation German-American married to a woman of Swiss-Norwegian descent, he was a goner before my toes cleared the wet stuff. Any way he matched up the fruit flies, he couldn't come up with *me*. Because my mom is one of those magic people with the natural capacity to make folks in shitty circumstances feel less shitty, she consoled Glenda and even brought her home until she could get her feet on the ground. Evidently Glenda was as surprised as Stephan; she'd had a one-night stand with my sperm donor to get even for a good thumping and had no idea the tall black-Japanese poet's squiggly swimmer was the one in a billion to crash through to the promised land.

Things sped rapidly downhill for Glenda as a single mother, and two years later, when she brought Child Protection Services crashing down on herself, getting heavily into crack and crank and heavily out of taking care of me, she remembered Mom's kindness, tracked her down and begged her to take me. Mom and Dad didn't blink—almost as if they were expecting me, to hear them tell it—and all of a sudden I was the rainbow-coalition kid of two white, upwardly mobile ex-children of the sixties.

Actually, only Mom was upwardly mobile. She's a lawyer, working for the assistant attorney general's office, mostly on child-abuse cases. Dad likes motorcycles; he's just mobile.

We never did hear from Glenda again, Mom says probably because the separation was too painful, and shameful.

Sometimes I find myself longing for her, just to see or talk with her, discover more about the unsettledness within me; but most of the time that ache sits in a shaded corner of my mind, a vague reminder of what it is not to be wanted. At the same time all that seems out of place, because I remember nothing about her, not what she looked like or the sound of her voice or even the touch of her hand. I do admit to having a few laughs imagining how history rewrote itself inside Stephan's head when my shiny brown head popped out.

It's interesting being "of color" in a part of the country where Mark Fuhrman has his own radio talk show. My parents have always encouraged me to be loud when I run into racism, but I can't count on racism being loud when it runs into me. Very few people come out and say they don't like you because you aren't white; when you're younger it comes at a birthday party you learn about after the fact, or later, having a girl say yes to a date only to come back after discussing it with her parents, having suddenly remembered she has another engagement that night. Not much to do about that but let it register and don't forget it. I learned in grade school that the color of a person's skin has to do only with where their way-long-ago ancestors originated, so my mind tells me all racists are either ignorant or so down on themselves they need somebody to be better than. Most of the time telling myself that works. Once in a while my gut pulls rank on my mind, and I'm compelled to get ugly.

I called "All News All Talk Radio" a couple of days after the first time I heard the spectacularly racially sensitive ex-L.A. detective giving Spokane and the rest of the Inland Empire the hot poop on big-time crime fighting. The talk

3

show I called had featured the mayors of an eastern Washington and a north Idaho town declaring that the racist label put on this region is undeserved, blown out of proportion due to the presence of the Aryan Nations fort over in Hayden Lake, Idaho, and the existence of several small militias spread out between central Washington and eastern Montana.

The mayors had departed when the talk-jock finally said, "We're talking with T. J. from Cutter, about fifty miles outside our great city."

I said, "So this racist label, it's undeserved?"

"I believe it is," he said. "An entire region can't be held responsible for the ignorant actions of a few. Certainly you can't argue with that."

"You're right," I said. "I can't. But if the racist label is about perceptions, and in this case, *undeserved* perceptions, why would you guys have the Mark Fuhrman show?"

"Have you tuned in to Mark's show?"

"Not purposely," I said, "but I was scanning the stations and landed right on him."

"How long did you listen?"

"Long enough to convince myself it was really him, that you guys weren't just pulling my chain."

"Then you heard a man who knows a lot about crime prevention and an accomplished professional radio man."

I said, "His voice was okay."

The jock said, "What's your point, T. J.?"

"That if you guys are running the most powerful AM station in the region and you're worried about people's perceptions of that region as racist, you might think twice before you give one of the true *icons* of racism in this country two hours of drive-time radio every week."

4

"We didn't hire Mark to talk about race relations. We hired him to talk about criminals and the criminal mind, and about the intricacies of police work. He's written books on the subject, you know."

"You didn't hire him because of his famous name?"

"No, sir, we did not."

"So when you decided your listeners needed to learn about Spokane, Washington, police work, you figured you'd get better expertise from a dishonored ex-L.A. cop rather than some retired veteran Spokane cop who might have covered Spokane's streets for twenty-five or thirty years?"

He said, "How old are you?"

"What does that matter?"

"You sound like a kid."

"You tell me why that matters, and I'll tell you how old I am."

"It matters because if you're too young, you might lack the experience to carry on this conversation intelligently."

"I'm a fifty-six-year-old retired Spokane policeman," I said, and paused a moment. "Guess I don't have the voice for it." I hung up.

I'm really not bothered by the race thing most of the time; at least I can say I don't bring it up first. And I've never wanted to be anyone else, and I don't want to be any other color. My bio-daddy must have had a pretty good brain because I have a big-time I.Q. and, Simet says, monster talent in articulation, plus I'm almost six-two and just a little under two hundred pounds. I can stuff a basketball from a standstill, and I've been clocked in a little over ten-point-four seconds for a hundred meters. When I was thirteen, I qualified for the Junior Olympics in two swimming events, and I'm even a pretty fair cowboy, having spent parts of three summers at Little Britches Rodeo Camp.

That's a pretty fair résumé for a guy who, until this year, never participated in one second of organized high school sports.

And I'm not hard to look at. Mr. Simet says I look like Tiger Woods on steroids, so I get plenty of chances to socialize. For every girl whose parents are terrified of a muddied gene pool, there's a girl who would use me as a threat to do just that. And there are plenty of girls who don't care one way or the other.

The truly unique thing about me isn't my racial heritage, or my brain or my size or my athletic abilities. Momma Glenda didn't leave me with much to remember her by, but she certainly left me with the all-time moniker. A lot of kids whose parents grew up in the hippie generation have names like Autumn or Somber or Twilight or Destiny. Who knows what their parents were smoking to name them after seasons or moods or times of day, but good old Glenda went them one better, naming me in her "spiritual" period. She may have been a little too "spiritual" on mood-altering funstuff to imagine my first day in kindergarten.

"Tell everyone your first name when your turn comes," Mrs. Herrick said, nodding to the pencil-necked, towheaded kid next to me. The kid said, "Roger."

I said, "The."

"Excuse me?"

"The." She should have said, "Tell everyone what people call you."

The other kids giggled. My fists clenched, blood rushing into my head.

Mrs. Herrick said, "Uh, do you have a middle name?"

"Tao," I said, pronouncing it correctly as "Dow."

6

"Your name is The Tao? What kind of name is that?"

I shrugged. "Mine."

To her credit, Mrs. Herrick glanced at her class roster to see if I was telling the truth and moved on, but as you might guess, that wasn't the end of it.

"It's a book," I told Sue Eldridge and Ronnie Blackburn later, my back against the jackets hanging on hooks at the rear of the room. I was as yet unaware it is also an entire philosophy.

"Why did your mother give you the same name as a book?" Sue asked.

"Just did." I wanted to explain that my *real* mother, Abby, didn't do that; that it was my buy-O mother, but I hadn't been real successful articulating that in the past.

Ronnie laughed and turned to the rest of the class, who were pulling on their coats for recess. "His mom gave him the same name as a book!" he yelled to them. Then a light clicked above his head. "Hey," he said, "me, too. My mom gave me the same name as a book, too. I'm Curious George!" He squealed in delight, falling to the floor between giggles, scratching under his arms like an ape.

Suddenly he was struggling to push my knee off his chest.

"Stop!" Mrs. Herrick yelled, but I punched Ronnie Blackburn in the nose anyway. It was the beginning of a series of unplanned three-day vacations that would dot my educational career like chicken pox.

But there's worse news about my handle, and if you've been paying attention, you know what it is: My health dictates the health of the nation's economy.

"How's your son doing, Mr. Jones?"

"The Tao's up today, sir."

7

"That's good news. Try to keep him happy."

Think I don't get carried away with those? To avoid confusion, and raucous laughter whenever my name is mentioned, I'm called T. J.

It's over now. I'm at the end of the summer following my senior year in high school; I have my diploma in a lockbox and the advantage of hindsight. But I want to tell it without that advantage—tell it as it unfolded—Mr. Simet says any story is only true in the moment.

My father always said there are no coincidences; that when two seemingly related events occur, they *are* related and should be treated that way. My father had very good reasons to try to understand how the universe works, which I'm sure I'll get into later.

The seemingly related things that I believe kick this story off happen on the second day of school. Coaches have tried to get me to turn out for sports since junior high. Sometimes they're insistent and sometimes downright nasty, accusing me of lacking the high school equivalent of patriotism, even to the point of calling me a traitor. But I've always eluded them. I'll play basketball three or four hours nonstop on open gym night, and I've always taken a couple of guys to Hoopfest in Spokane, which is the largest three-on-three street-basketball tournament in the country, and my team has won its division every time. I think I could have been a pretty fair football player; I'm sure not afraid to take a hit or to put a good lick on a guy, but something inside me recoils at being told what to do, and that doesn't sit well with most coaches, who are paid to do exactly that. I don't blame them; I know it's me. But the better you know yourself, the better chance you have of staying clear of trouble, and I'm pretty sure I'd never have lasted a full season of football with Coach Benson or basketball with Coach Roundtree. At one point or another in the heat of a game, Benson and Roundtree retreat to the time-tested and highly grating tool of public humiliation as a motivator, and that particular tool brings me back in your face faster than a yo-yo on a bungee cord, at which time I immediately suspend the notion of giving a shit.

So why was I considering joining a swim team that didn't exist before this year when I haven't been competitive in the water since fourteen, except for trying to beat Dad into the shower every morning? It's Simet. He catches me after third-period English and says, "Jones, didn't you used to be a pretty good swimmer?"

"I'm still a pretty good swimmer," I say. "Wanna try me?" Simet and I enjoy a longstanding rivalry wherein one of us challenges the other to some athletic contest. We handicap it based on our abilities (he lies like a student with a term paper due to get an advantage) and then make a friendly wager, say my English grade against some unsavory task he needs done, like stirring his compost heap when the temperature rises above eighty, or washing and waxing his Humvee, which looks better dirty.

He says, "I want to try you, but not against me."

"Who?"

"Someone different every week."

Visions of age-group swimming pop up: permanently chlorinated hair and eyes, clogged sinuses, ear infections. "This has a familiar ring."

"What do you think?"

"That you generally give me less information than I need to make an informed decision."

9

He gathers his books and nods toward the parking lot. "Hop into my babe-mobile and I'll buy you a milk shake. Maybe a pizza. We'll talk."

I follow him down the hall. "Make it a steak. Something is sick and wrong here."

"Let's hope it takes you awhile to figure out what it is."

At Solomon's Pizza, Simet tells me that Mr. Morgan, the principal, asked him to replace Mr. Packenbush as assistant wrestling coach, who's resigning due to reasons of health. In a burst of panic, Simet told Morgan he's been trying to get a swimming team going, since Cutter is one of only three high schools in the conference without one.

I say, "Morgan, of course, pointed out that we don't have a pool."

"Way ahead of him," he says back. "I told him I could get free workout time at All Night Fitness, which I'm praying will actually be true."

"The pool at All Night is twenty yards," I remind him, "with an underwater ledge at the shallow end that will give you a subdural hematoma if you flip your turn." A subdural hematoma is what happens to your brain if you get whacked on the head hard enough to bounce it off the inside of your skull. I hear that term a lot when my mom is trying a child-abuse case.

Simet says I'm mucking things up with details—

"With only four lanes—"

—making it more difficult than it had to be.

"—and a ladder smack in the middle of one of them."

I should think of it as a challenge.

"Every meet would be away," I tell him. "No teams would come here to swim. In a twenty-yard pool, records don't count."

10

"All part of what makes an insurmountable obstacle interesting," he says. "A perennial road team. Mermen without a pond."

"You're forgetting something else. Nobody I swam with in age-group swimming lives here. There can't be three real swimmers in this entire school."

He considers that a minute, takes a bite of pizza and a long swallow on his beer. "I'm going off the record here," he says. "Educators are supposed to stick together and not bad-mouth one another, so we can collectively stay ahead of the educatees. But do you know Coach Murphy?"

Murphy is sixty-eight years old, having received divine dispensation to teach till two days after he dies, and I have judiciously avoided taking PE or health classes from him for four years. He tolerates zero bullshit or less. "Yeah, I know Coach Murphy."

"Then you know what my life would be like as his assistant." He leans forward. "I have my ways, Jones. If I go down, you go with me, which is to say if I coach wrestling, you wrestle. You have completed six semesters of English. You need eight. Think how easy it would be for me to misplace your records a week before graduation or remove a leg from one of your A's. You'd be caught at Cutter High School like a rat in a Twilight Zone cage."

"They're really willing to let you have this team? No facility, no swimmers?"

"One swimmer," he says.

"One used-to-be swimmer," I say back.

"T. J., I've looked at some of your old times. You were phenomenal. And I've coached some big-time swimmers, guys headed for the trials. Tell you what, I can whip you into good-enough shape to get us points at State, which

11

would elevate Cutter in the overall all-sport state championship."

"Spock, are you out of your Vulcan mind?" I ask in my best William Shatner, which isn't all that bad.

Simet fixes his gaze on the table. "Actually, that's why they agreed. I told them you were a lock. If I don't come through, they'll sue for malpractice."

"You mean if *I* don't come through, they'll sue for malpractice."

"Same thing."

"If it's the same thing, you swim."

He nods at the remaining slice of pizza and says, "Go ahead and eat that," which means he is desperate. He glances at his watch as I snap it up. "You don't have to answer tonight. I'll give you twelve hours."

It could be worse. Simet is a guy who always teaches you something, and it's not always about English or journalism. He *was* a hell of a swimmer himself in his younger years, when dinosaurs roamed the planet, and he seldom lets his classes forget what a spiritual experience it is to test yourself against that particular element. And though I burned out on it back then, I remember what amazing solace I felt working out. Up until I started swimming in grade school, half my teachers wanted me medicated and the other half wanted me in reform school. It helped me focus, beveled the edges on my boundless, uncontrolled energy, dulled my rage. All things considered, it is enough to make me consider Simet's proposal.

And here comes the kicker, the thing my father would say couldn't be a coincidence. I'm walking out of Simet's room the next day, thinking if I go along with him, I'll be breaking a career-long rule banning myself from organized sports while playing as many disorganized sports as time in my life allows. I mean, I *love* athletics. When I'm gliding to the hoop in a pickup game, or gunning some guy down at home plate from center field in a summer vacant-lot game, or falling into a perfect pace five miles out on a run, I feel downright godlike. But those things I do on my own. Cutter is *such* a jock school; they pray before games and cajole you to play out of obligation, and fans scream obscenities at one another from the stands, actually creating rivalries between *towns*, which has always seemed crazy to me. I remember my freshman year when the entire town was actually happy because the stud running back from Jackson Quarry became ineligible because of grades. Our *educational* community got giddy because some kid they didn't know tanked his math class. I mean, fifteen seconds after I finish a three-on-three game at Hoopfest, I'm sitting on the curb sharing Gatorade with the guys on the other team, talking about moves they put on me, and vice versa. Why would anyone want his opponent not to be at his best?

I'm on a roll there, but the point is that athletics has become such a big thing here that our administration begins each year figuring ways to pile up points for this all-sport state championship. And the symbol, the Shroud of Turin for Cutter High athletes, is the letter jacket. A block C on a blue-and-gold leather-and-wool jacket at Cutter High School is worth a whole bunch of second chances in the front office, of which I'm still waiting for my first. Those who don't own one of those jackets can easily become victims of our zero-tolerance policy. Well, in the eyes of The Tao Jones, nothing is true without its opposite, and it has been my minor quest to make sure that the finest athlete at Cutter High School did his very best to never earn that jacket. I should also say I'm not *totally* righteous in my quest for athletic purity. When I was an age-group swimmer I was *driven*. It consumed me, and I get uneasy thinking of becoming that focused on it again.

Variation on the theme. I'm moving catlike through the halls toward my locker minutes after Simet has challenged me to become the Mark Spitz of the desert (we don't have a *swimming pool*) and run into Mike Barbour—linebacker extraordinaire and student most likely to graduate with multiple felonies—jacking up Chris Coughlin against the lockers by the drinking fountain because Chris is wearing his dead brother's letter jacket.

Chris Coughlin is big-time special ed. He's main-streamed into PE and industrial arts, but spends most of his time in Resource Room improving his reading skills enough to read traffic signs and memorizing the intricacies of basic addition and subtraction. Everyone knows Chris's story: born addicted to crack cocaine, then got a double dose of shit just after his first birthday when his mother's boyfriend wrapped his face in Saran Wrap to make him stop crying. At his sentencing the boyfriend said he only wanted to make Chris pass out, not cause permanent brain damage. Oops.

Anyway, Chris's aunt and uncle took him and did all they could to make it up to him, but they couldn't regenerate brain cells. Chris's older half-brother, Brian, was raised by his own biological father and is something of a legend around Cutter from four or five years ago for having gained more yards in football and for hitting more home runs in baseball than any Cutter Wolverine before or since, and for being drafted into the Cincinnati Reds farm system out of

14

high school. He was destined to have a street or a small park named after him someday, but was killed in a freak rock-climbing accident in the spring of his senior year. That about did poor old Chris in. He didn't have much, but he had a famous big brother. Brian was a real class act: good student, good athlete, great guy. The only times I remember seeing Chris smile were when he rode behind Brian on his dirt bike, or later, after Brian was gone, when he'd brag to anyone who would listen every time he passed Brian's picture in the trophy case. They didn't live together, but Brian sure let everyone know Chris was his brother, and if you messed with Chris back in those days—he was an easy mark—you could expect a visit from Brian.

So Barbour has the jacket buttoned at the bottom and pulled down around Chris's shoulders so he can't move his arms, and his nose is about an inch from Chris's. I can't hear what he's saying, but tears squirt out of Chris's terrified eyes and his entire body trembles. I hustle over and insert myself between them, put an arm over Chris's shoulder, and say, "What's the matter, buddy? You look like you've been staring into a giant asshole," and move him a few steps down the hall, adjusting the jacket. Chris is hyperventilating, barely able to breathe.

"When you see one of those," I tell him, loud enough for Barbour to hear, "you gotta close your eyes and pretend it's not there. Course it helps if you also hold your breath."

Barbour's hand clamps onto my shoulder, and I turn in mock surprise. "Barbour! 'Sup, man?"

"I was talking to him, shithead."

"That's Mister Shithead to you. You were talking to my buddy Chris? He has to get to class. I run his complaint department, though, right, Chris?"

Still speechless, Chris nods.

Barbour says, "Fine. I'll tell you. Next time I see him in this jacket, I'll take it off him and burn it. You earn one of these if you're gonna wear it at this school, something you're too chicken shit to know anything about. It's an honor to wear these colors. You don't put on the jacket your brother earned. That's an athletic department rule."

I say, "Doesn't apply. Chris isn't *in* the athletic department," and Barbour says, "Yeah, well, in this school an athletic department rule is a school rule."

"Guess that wasn't in my orientation packet," I say. "What's the matter with you, Barbour? You know the deal with Coughlin's brother. Is this *prick* thing habitual, or do you work at it?"

"One of these days you're going to find out, Jones."

"I lie awake nights, waiting for that day."

Barbour says, "I'll save my energy for a white man."

"Because of your limited I.Q. I'll give you one of those, my friend. One more will get us both a three-day suspension." Barbour's family is famous for their send-all-the-Japs-back-to-Japan-with-a-nigger-under-each-arm attitude, so I feel like I have to hold my own.

We stand facing each other a few seconds, and finally Barbour reiterates the athletic department's zero-tolerance position on letter jackets and walks away. I pat Chris's shoulder and tell him not to worry about it and start for class, but look back to see him stuffing the jacket into his locker, trying in vain to cram it behind his books.

I walk back, pull the jacket out, and hand it to him. "Chris, you can wear it. It's okay."

"He said it was a rule."

"He lied. You can wear it anytime you want."

16

"He said the athletic department gots a rule."

"It belonged to your brother, Chris. You wear it. If Barbour gives you any more trouble, you come tell me, okay?"

Chris stares at me.

"Okay?"

"Okay." He says it without conviction.

As I turn the corner for class, I glance back again, and Coughlin is frantically stuffing the jacket back into the locker.

I stay in the afternoon to catch up on an article for the school paper, and catch a flash of blue and gold as I pass the janitor emptying the day's leavings into the Dumpster. I wait until he moves back inside and take a look, and sure enough, drag a Cutter High letter jacket out, with COUGHLIN lettered across the back.

Later I drive over to All Night Fitness to see if there is *any* possibility I can train in that pool. We have a family membership, so I spend time there already, but almost never in the water. Since it's the only indoor pool in town, All Night rents it out for parties and YMCA swim lessons and women's and seniors' water aerobics classes. I hope to swim a few laps to get a feel, but a sign on the entrance says PRIVATE GROUP. I push the swinging door open and stand just inside.

A young man and woman in Y T-shirts stand with lifeguard poles at either side of the pool, and Y staff people are spread out through the crowd like Secret Service at the White House Easter Egg Roll. Political correctness aside, the water and deck are filled with kids who look like they'll be getting the very best parking places for the rest of their lives. In the far lane Chris Coughlin helps a little girl with shriveled arms on a kickboard. The girl locks her gnarled elbows over the Styrofoam board and kicks while Chris pulls her along. The noise is deafening, but I watch him patiently help her extend her feet, toes pointed inward to propel herself properly, then release the board long enough to let her move under her own power for a few kicks until she becomes still in the water. Then he pulls her a little farther. I am struck with how completely comfortable he seems in the water.

His brother's jacket is still in my car, and I intend to go get it, but when I yell to get his attention he glances up, then quickly away, and I know my presence embarrasses him, so I just wave. He looks ashamed. How messed up is that? You get treated like shit, then have to be ashamed that you're the kind of person people treat like shit.

I stay a few minutes, imagining myself trying to get a decent workout in that abbreviated pool. It doesn't look promising. But as I drive through the quiet dusky streets of the uncharacteristically warm Cutter fall, Chris's ease in the water flashes before me and suddenly the mathematics—the *relativity*—of it all hits me. If it kills Barbour to see a guy as far out of the mainstream as Chris is, wearing a letter jacket that doesn't belong to him, how far up his nose will it get when he sees him wearing one that *does* belong to him? And suddenly I hear the voice the universe—and Simet—wants me to hear. It says, "Swim."

2

Among his many other quirks, my father, John Paul Jones, is a TV buff. He doesn't sit around staring at it all day, but he religiously records certain programs to watch later. Usually they are jock interviews or hourlong biographies or educational TV documentaries about animals whose faces are carbon copies of their asses, or about black holes and the Hubble space telescope and *anything* about whales.

One interview Dad watches over and over, and believes should be shown at the beginning of every athletic season at Cutter High School and to every coach and administrator and athlete who ever hears the cheers of his hometown crowd, is an interview that Roy Firestone of ESPN did with Arthur Ashe not long before the tennis great died of AIDS. Ol' Roy was the king of drawing tears, but he was way out of his league because if anyone ever got tears out of Arthur Ashe, they would *never* be tears for himself. So after several attempts, Roy leaned forward and said, "Arthur, when you're all alone, do you ever just look up and say, 'Why me?' "

Arthur looked him straight in the eye, and in that soft, steady voice that came to represent the very meaning of integrity before his death, said, "Why not me?"

Dad says Arthur knew something that eludes most of the jocks and coaches and administrators at Cutter: that the universe doesn't create special dispensation for a guy because he can run faster or jump higher or thread the needle with a fastball. He knew that we take what the universe gives us, and we either get the most out of it or we don't, but in the end we all go out the same way.

So I hang back after Simet's class while he's gathering our papers off his desk.

"Don't leave me hanging, Jones. Morgan is closing in on me about the wrestling position. He says with the shortage of male teachers this year, we're all drawing extra duty."

"The testosterone shuffle."

He picks up his grade book. "Let's see, how are you doing in my class?"

I say, "I'll do it."

"My God." He stares, eyes following his finger across the page. "Straight A's. What a guy."

"But I won't do it alone."

"I'll be with you every stroke of the way."

"That's not what I mean. I know you swam on a small college team," I say, "but not so small the workouts were solitary confinement. I need a team around me."

"Better start recruiting."

"I'm ahead of you. Only scouted one guy so far, but there have to be more where he came from. I mean, we evolved from water, right?"

"That's right," he says. "Swimmers under every rock."

"One other thing. Who establishes the criteria to earn a letter?"

"The coach of the sport," he says. "Why? You think I'd let you jerk me out from in front of the oncoming grapplers' train and not give you a letter? What kind of man do you think I am?"

"Never mind that, but I'm not thinking of me. I want whoever else I get to come overboard with me to have a chance."

"When I see the caliber of fish you're catching, we'll talk about it."

Whatever caliber of fish I catch, they'll all be suckers, but no sense getting into that with him yet.

A lot happens in my imagination. In my imagination Chris Coughlin stands in front of his locker in his own letter jacket, a miniature gold swimmer stroking across the middle of the C, and when some righteous buttmunch like Mike Barbour jacks him up, some *ultra*-righteous coach, say maybe Simet, has Barbour running stairs.

And in my imagination I have answers to the pertinent questions, such as, "Who else can I get to piss off the likes of Mike Barbour?" And *some*times what is in my imagination comes to fruition. See, by the time most of us get to ninth grade, we know whether we can play football or basketball or baseball—the big three—or whether we're fast enough or can jump high or far enough to turn out for track. But no way do we know our talents as swimmers. I mean, most Cutter kids swim and water ski on the river, so a lot of us can propel ourselves in a life jacket from the place we fall to the ski, but when I swam age group, my parents drove me a good forty-five minutes to the nearest indoor pool. The point is, there have to be at least a few other guys around like Chris Coughlin, with that natural feel for the water, who we can recruit to keep me from looking like the national swim team for Antarctica.

Swimming's a winter sport in high school, so I have some time to pull it all together, but swimming's also a sport you train long and hard for if you don't want to embarrass yourself in a big way when your stroke falls apart on the final lap of a two-hundred free because you haven't put in the requisite miles, so I can't wait too long.

The following weekend I run off about fifty envelopes I designed on Mom's computer. They say YOU MAY HAVE ALREADY WON! with a reproduction of Ed McMahon and Dick Clark in one corner. Then I stuff a flyer inside that reads FEARLESS HIGH SCHOOL MERMEN & MERMAIDS WANTED: CASH PRIZES AND INSTANT FAME above my telephone number, and because we are having one of those rare great hot fall days, I take them out to the river and stick one under the windshield wiper of every car in sight. I figure, hey, it's a river. At least most of the people here can swim.

Eight hours later, in the early evening, I answer the phone to the first ring and hear, "To whom might I be speaking?"

I say, "Shouldn't that be my question?"

"It might be if you hadn't left a number without a name on that flyer you placed on my automobile windshield this afternoon."

"This is T. J. Jones." I do know that's redundant, by the way: the J and the Jones. "And to whom might I be speaking?" I ask, placing the "m" on the end of *who* for what I hope will be the last time in my history of casual speech.

"You might be speaking to almost anyone, as many of those flyers as you distributed," the voice says, "but you *are* speaking to Daniel Hole."

When your name is The Tao Jones, you think twice before passing judgment on a peer's name, but I am quick with silent gratitude that my last name can't be translated into any target so basic to adolescent males. "What can I do for you, Mr. Hole?"

"I called to gather information regarding your rallying

22

cry for fearless swimmers. I'm assuming you're in search of people who experience a certain amount of comfort in the water."

Dan Hole. He was in my English class a few years ago, and I think a couple of social studies classes since. Dan "Never-Use-a-Single-Syllable-When-Polysyllables-Are-Available" Hole. I say, "Yeah, people who experience comfort in the water. Is that you?"

"Totally comfortable," he says. "What is your plan?"

"My plan?"

"Well, do you simply want to acquaint yourself with people who can swim, or is there some mission?"

Jesus. "We need you for a swim team."

Silence fills the line.

"Dan?"

After a moment, "That would require a considerable outlay of energy."

"And time," I say.

"Indeed." More silence. "I actually participated on a swimming team in my youth," he says.

"That's great," I say back. "Exactly what we're looking for."

Dan wants particulars. Where will we swim; when? Will the chlorine level be controlled better than it was at the YMCA pool in his former hometown, where he swam for their team? (I assure him it will, at which time he questions my sincerity, given I don't even know where his former hometown is, and therefore cannot possibly have the particulars on the chemical makeup of the water in the YMCA there. I lie and say all YMCAs are the same; it's a rule.) Will we have time for our homework? One doesn't ever want to get out of balance with the "athletic thing," as many of the football players are wont to do. I assure him I'm interested in a college education myself and wouldn't go out for a sport where I might be wont to not want to do my homework. That seems to satisfy him. "And our mentor would be whom?"

"You mean the coach?"

"Yes, the coach."

I say it would be Simet.

Another silence.

"He's my English teacher," I tell him.

"Yes, I'm aware of Mr. Simet. He's rather frivolous, don't you think?"

I agree Simet can be a bit of a slacker, but I assure Dan Hole he was a collegiate swimmer and is probably the best we can do under the circumstances. Dan is wearing off on me. I say *collegiate.*

"Let me get back to you on this," Dan says. "I'm tempted to respond to impulse and sign on, but history tells me that's ill-advised. I'll have a reply within forty-eight hours."

I hang up, exhausted.

I know if I end up with Chris Coughlin and Dan Hole, seemingly two ends of some otherworldly continuum, I'll need to get some guys to fill in the middle, if for no other reason than to save Chris.

The second call comes from Tay-Roy Kibble. Tay-Roy is a guy I know from every school musical production from grade school tonette band to high school symphony, choral events included. This guy has a set of pipes on him, and plays all the woodwind instruments, plus the piano, well enough to be presented as a featured soloist every time. He's also a bodybuilder, though not quite as accomplished there as in the musical field. He doesn't embarrass himself, though, and enters only steroid-free events, usually placing in the top five of eighteen-and-unders. Tay-Roy is a senior, too.

On the phone he says, "This is Tay-Roy Kibble. I'm calling about a flyer on my car windshield out at the river this morning."

"Hey, Tay-Roy. T. J. Jones. I'm trying to get enough guys together for a school swim team. Mr. Simet wants to coach it . . . actually, to keep from having to be an assistant wrestling coach." I go on to give him the downside: no real pool, all "away" meets, basically giving him every excuse to say, "Excuse me, my Caller ID shows an important call" and unplug his phone, because I know the hours he puts into his music, not to mention the bodybuilding.

"Actually, that sounds kind of fun. I'm kinda burned out on the bodybuilding thing. You have to travel too far to catch the drug-free contests, and the price of regular supplements is killing me."

I ask if he swims much.

"I can chase down my water ski," he says, laughing. "Actually, I swam the river, over and back, from Boulder Beach last summer."

That isn't bad. It's more than three-quarters of a mile across there. I tell him that's farther than I've swum in the last year and sign him up. If nothing else, Tay-Roy is plenty familiar with All Night Fitness. When he's working out for a contest, he'll spend more time on that little bump of a muscle that pops out right next to your elbow than I spend on my entire upper body. He even knows what that muscle is called.

So if I can convince Chris to swim, and Dan assesses the

25

situation in our favor, we'll have at least enough swimmers for a relay. Who knows what else will come floating up from the bottom?

My quest gains momentum the next day while I'm pitching the team one more time to Chris Coughlin at first lunch, and look up to see Barbour standing over us with a couple of offensive (I won't say *how* offensive) linemen. Talk about thinking football is *life*. Cutter could win it all this year, and football guys are gods. Before the first game is even played, Barbour is being talked about as first string All-State. The one thing that could make me play football is if I could transfer to another school and go up against that asshole. Anyway, it's clear he's going to loom until I acknowledge his presence, but I leave him unattended until Chris appears ready to bolt out of sheer terror. "Barbour the Barbarian," I say finally. "What can I do for you?"

"I wanna talk to the dummy."

I point to Greg Steelman, the lineman beside him. "So talk."

He points to Chris. "That dummy."

"Christopher may not be matriculating to Harvard," I say, "but he's plenty smart enough not to waste his time in discourse with you. What do you want?" *Matriculating. Discourse.* Dan Hole is lodged in my brain.

He glares at Chris. "I said I was—"

I stand, shoving my chair back hard enough to send it crashing to the floor—bringing us into focus as objects of attention from five tables in every direction—then step forward. Steelman puts a hand on my shoulder, but I brush it off with enough force to let him know he'll at least get his hair messed up messing with me. "If you call my friend a

26

dummy one more time, I'm going to take you apart. I know, you're a hotshot football stud and you think nobody has your number, but even if I don't, we go at it, we get three days to cool off, and that means you miss three days of practice, which makes you ineligible for the game Friday. It makes me ineligible for a math test. So go ahead, Barbour, sound off." I think I said I've spent a record number of days out of school for letting the heat that starts in my gut rise all the way, and I do my best to keep that under control, but the day I take Barbour out will be worth finishing the year homeschooled.

Coach Benson, the head football coach, spots us from his lunch-duty spot by the door and hustles over. "What's going on?"

"I'm just keeping these two apprised of the school athletic code; how nobody wears a letter jacket but the guy who earns it."

I translate that for Benson. "He wants to tell Chris Coughlin one more time he can't wear his dead brother's jacket."

Chris puts his head down, and I touch his shoulder. "Sorry, buddy, I shouldn't have said it like that."

"There's pride in being an athlete at this school."

"There may have been before you peed into the athletic gene pool," I tell him.

Coach Benson says, "Mr. Jones, there's no call for that kind of language."

"I'm just speaking in his native tongue, sir." I realize I stepped onto dangerous ground with Benson, who is a stickler for courteous language, so I follow with, "Sorry, sir. You're right. What I should have said is that Barbour is a stud football player with everything going for him, and it ticks me off when he takes after somebody like my friend Chris, who has a tough time protecting himself."

Coach looks at Barbour.

"I didn't take after anybody," Barbour says. "Like I said, I was just bringing these guys up to speed on the letter jacket rule. Just the stuff we talked about in the Lettermen's Club meeting."

Benson is the adviser for the Lettermen's Club, so whatever they talked about, he knows.

I put my arm over Chris's shoulder. He's wearing an old Levi's jacket, nearly worn through at the elbows, which couldn't have been washed since he entered high school. "This isn't a letter jacket," I say. Chris stands silent beside me, eyes darting like it's his first day on the prison yard. I say, "Hey, man, take off, okay? I'll catch up with you later. And we're agreed, right? You're gonna swim?"

"Maybe," he says. "It sounds hard."

I say, "Very soft. The water's very soft."

He laughs.

When Chris is out of earshot, I turn back to Barbour.

"I caught him wearing his brother's jacket again at the bowling alley last night," Barbour says. "What kind of pride can we have if—"

I say, "Coach, I don't want to be disrespectful with the language again, so I might need a little help with this. What's an acceptable term for chicken shit?"

"You're on thin ice, Jones."

I take a deep breath. Even Benson has to be reasonable on this one, if I don't push him any further into Barbour's camp. "Okay, what's an acceptable term for a big-time football hero who's threatened by a brain-damaged kid so scared he can barely make it through a school day without

28

hyperventilating himself into unconsciousness, wearing his dead brother's letter jacket because it's the only thing that gives him any connection to his brother and therefore to this school?"

Coach scratches his chin. Interesting how you can say almost anything you want as long as you don't say shit or fuck or any word derivative thereof. I'm getting a handle on the communication thing. He says, "I'll admit it's a different situation with the Coughlin kid, but the jacket is a symbol of excellence. The Lettermen's Club and the school Athletic Council have adopted a zero-tolerance policy on this."

I'm speechless a second; it doesn't fit that a grown man could be that dumb. I say, "What do the Lettermen's Club and the Athletic Council have to do with making school policy? They have an administration for that. They have a school board."

"That's true, Jones. But in case you haven't noticed, Cutter High School lives and dies on its athletic reputation. Eighty or ninety percent of the respect shown this school is for its athletic accomplishments."

"Shown by *who?*"

"By other schools, by townspeople who vote on tax levies and make other kinds of financial contributions. Believe me, Jones, the athletic department in this school has plenty of power—which, by the way, you could have shared in, had you had any school spirit. You could be wearing one of these jackets, Jones."

"Coach, I wouldn't wear the same brand of *underwear* Mike Barbour wears." This seems like a good time to back out of this conversation, so as not to tip my hand. I say, "I don't know if you heard Barbour correctly a minute ago, but he said he saw Chris wearing Brian's jacket in a *bowling alley*. That's completely away from school. Any chance we can keep this zero-tolerance thing confined to the grounds?"

I don't wait for the answer, just pick up my backpack and head across the lunchroom.

Coach Benson is an interesting case. Things are black and white with him. He can't understand why I won't play football and basketball for Cutter. I sat down and explained it to him once, told him how ugly I get when people start yelling and telling me what to do, but he said I was immature, that someday I would look back and regret not giving what I had to my school. He's not the real enemy here. You have to admire the consistency in his life. He played three sports here at Cutter, was a standout defensive back at a small college in Montana, and came right back here to coach. He married his college sweetheart, and they've been together since. He goes to church, takes charge when any family in town experiences a crisis. I mean, you can't dislike the guy, even when he blurts out his "zero-tolerance" policy on letter jackets. On the other hand, what kind of person has time to dream up a zero-tolerance policy on *letter jackets*?

After school I catch up with Chris again. Actually, he catches up with me hanging out in the journalism room trying to outsmart the Internet controls the school puts on to keep us on the straight and narrow as we travel the information highway. I've just typed in "chicken breasts," hoping the browser will spit back a little bit about chickens and a whole lot about breasts.

"What are you doing?"

I swivel in the computer chair; Chris is staring at the screen. "Medical research," I say, clicking Exit. "What are *you* doing?"

He shrugs, glances uneasily at the door.

"You worried about Barbour? The football guys?"

He glances at the door again. "A little bit."

I tell him this is the safest part of the day. "This is when we know exactly where all those gorillas are. They're out on the football field."

Chris laughs. "Gorillas."

I say, "Big hairy gorillas in shoulder pads," and he laughs louder. "In jock straps," and he squeals. It's like playing with a little kid. I say, "Look, Chris, I have an idea. Your brother was a pretty big guy, right?"

"Yeah, he was big. Way big. He played football. And baseball. He gots drafted . . ." He hesitates, and tears of remembrance rim his eyes.

"I know, Chris. Everyone remembers your brother. They have his picture in the trophy case so we won't forget."

He launches into all the statistics next to Brian's picture, but I stop him. "I know, Chris. I read it every day, just like you do."

He looks around the room and moves closer and in a near-whisper says, "I don't really read it; some of the words are too hard."

I say, "Yeah, but you know what it says, right?"

He smiles. "Right."

"Okay, here's my idea. Your brother was big, and you're not quite so big."

He smiles.

"So actually the jacket doesn't fit you very well. I mean, when you wear it, I can't even see your hands."

"I think I'm not going to wear it. Those football guys said they was gonna burn it."

I say, "Yeah, that wouldn't be good. Listen, now that you're going to be a swimmer—"

He smiles. "I'm gonna be a swimmer in the soft water."

"Right. Now that you're going to be a swimmer in the soft water, we've got to have a way to identify you; you know, like let everyone know you're a swimmer. I've got a great jacket at home that doesn't fit me anymore. It has a big Speedo emblem on the back. Speedo is a company that makes swimming suits and goggles and stuff that swimmers wear. How about I give you that one, and you keep your brother's jacket safe at home? You could put it someplace in your room where you can look at it every day. And then you can come to school in the Speedo jacket and everyone will know you're a stud swimmer."

He laughs again, as if he's never considered the idea of Chris Coughlin, the stud.

He isn't alone.

Boys' sports at Cutter High School are driven by the downtown alumni, who call themselves "Wolverines Too,"
almost as much as it's driven by the athletic department, or
by Mr. Morgan, the principal. That bothers me because the
power behind Wolverines Too is a guy I *never* forget to keep
my eye out for. His name is Rich Marshall, and he eats
what he finds dead in the road. Supposedly WT is a group of
community-spirited Cutter graduates who hung around
after graduation to make their fortunes in this mountain
town of nine thousand people just far enough north of
Spokane to be Hick City. In theory, their organization sup-
ports all Cutter extracurricular activities. That should
encompass music, drama, honors society, the chess club,
and, in my book, the kids who hang out on the smoking
hill. In fact, it encompasses male jocks. Wolverines Too is
basically a group of guys whose glory days unfolded on the
Cutter athletic arena between the ages of fourteen and
eighteen and who want to re-create those glory days
through the lives of Cutter's current stable of jocks. They
"mentor" them, and sometimes find them jobs in their
places of work. They've been known to raise significant
dollars for football equipment or basketball uniforms when
allocated athletic funds run low. In my memory they have
never raised a dime for a girls' team. I find it interesting
that not one former *female* athlete belongs to the group.

Rich Marshall encompasses most of what I believe is wrong with our species, and I don't say that just because of his family's civil-rights record, which is not unlike the Barbours'. The entire Marshall family operates in a permanent state of confusion because they can't figure out who they hate most. Rich graduated the year before I started high school, so by all rights I should have never had contact with him, but a year after he graduated, his dad died of a heart attack and Rich took over Marshall Logging, which is probably one of the few viable logging companies left in the Northwest. Mike Barbour sets chokers for them in the summer at about three or four times minimum wage. I swear, Barbour's the only guy I know with a full ride to high school.

Rich and I got crossways of each other when I was a freshman, after he shot a deer out from under me.

Let me back up a bit and say I don't get it about guns and male bonding and becoming one with your father or uncle by killing some animal born unfortunate enough not to know what a malevolent subspecies the human predator is. To quote my favorite philosopher, Chris Rock, "What kind of ignorant shit is that?" I think people don't consider sometimes how *arbitrary* things are. If this country had been founded by photographers, fathers and sons could bind their connections bringing back *pictures* of the animals they now bring draped over the hoods of their four-wheel-drive pickups. They could do that now if they understood that the whole hunting thing got started back before you could get meat at a drive-up window. But when an activity has outlived its usefulness in this country, we keep it alive by calling it a sport. It's a *sport* to drive to the edge of the woods and fire a nine-hundred-mile-an-hour missile that tears a hole in its target before that target even hears the crack of the rifle. Listen, if you want to make a sport of deer hunting, take any weapon no sharper than an antler, chase it down, and get it on. Yeah, yeah, the deer would then have the advantage of speed, but you'd still have the overwhelming advantage of malicious intent.

A digression into politics there, but I'm better now.

I was recounting how I got on the bad side of Rich Marshall, as if there were a good side. I was a freshman, hanging out at Durfee's Chevron with a bunch of guys my age, drinking pop and listening to heroic stories about their first football season, which they were in the middle of. It was the final weekend of deer-hunting season. Rich had already decided Barbour was going to replace him as Jabba the Jock and had taken him under his wing like out of some United Way Big Brother from a negative universe. Rich and Mike and Mark Wyberg roared into the station in Rich's big ol' Ford dualie, one of those monster pickup trucks that runs on diesel, with dual wheels in the rear and a camper on the back he still claims every cheerleader in school has been naked in. I swear, if God had made Rich choose between that ugly truck and his you-know-what, which he claims is also supersized by McDonald's, it would have been a three-day decision. Anyway, he stormed into the front office yelling, "Any you guys not got your deer yet?"

There was no *yet* for me. No one who values longevity would bring an animal he just shot for kicks into *my* mother's kitchen. Marshall pulled a twenty out of his wallet. "One a' you guys run down to Bender's Sports and get you a tag," he said. "Quick."

I asked why.

"Got us a little one tied up out there," he said. "Nailed his momma, and the dumb little shitter just stood there. So we lassoed him, cowboy style, but we can't chance bringin' him out with no tag. Fish an' Game boys all over the damn place. I can talk 'em out of him bein' too small if I got a tag on 'im; just say he was a long ways off an' I misjudged. Gonna take that bad boy over to Hoyt's Taxidermy an' have 'im stuffed. Put 'im in the yard come Christmas."

I feigned interest long enough to get the approximated coordinates of the doomed Bambi, then said no chance was I going to get a deer tag so these erstwhile frontiersmen could gun down a baby deer with a rope around his neck, courageous as that sounded.

Rich looked like he might use my head for a speed bag when I started humming "Davy Crockett," but one of the other guys offered to go to Bender's. It was never a bad idea to build up a few points with Rich; he had graduated the previous year and, as part of his commitment to Wolverines Too, was donating time to work out with the team, and you just might end up staring across the line at him in some practice drill designed to make you eligible for state disability funds.

Anyway, while Marshall and his Gang of Two drove Ralph Raymond to Bender's, I pedaled my mountain bike out past the old Carter place deep into the woods on an overgrown one-lane logging road to a clearing where, sure enough, the young deer stood vigil over his dead mother, a nylon rope snug around his neck, tied to a pine tree. This wasn't just Bambi, this was *early* Bambi. Mom and Dad said later it may have had to do with the loss of my own mother, but I'll never forget the look of it, head bowed, standing over her still corpse. I could almost feel the weight in its chest in my own.

The fawn lurched as I rode up, choking on the tightened noose, but I laid my bike on the ground, talking real soft as

I moved in, and though it jerked back in panic twice more, I was able to slip the rope over its head. It bounded away a few yards, stopped, and ventured back. I knew Marshall couldn't be far behind, so I yelled and whistled and even slapped it on the butt, but it never got past the edge of the trees before turning back.

Across the clearing a cloud of dust rolled up behind Rich's dualie as he slammed on the brakes, snatched his rifle from the gun rack as he leaped from the cab and sprinted toward me and the deer with Wyberg and Barbour close behind, screaming my name.

Even with all that commotion the fawn wouldn't go far, and there was nothing left but to throw myself over it. To shoot the deer, asshole Rich Marshall would have to shoot me, and in my imagination that would be better than to witness this killing. Wyberg and Barbour tried to peel me back, slapping the back of my head and kicking my ribs, and in the chaos the deer kicked a three-inch gash in my forehead, but I held on like a bulldogger and Rich couldn't get a clean body shot. I will forever remember the sensation of that animal going slack in my hold as the bullet went through his temple.

Then the three of them proceeded to kick my ass all over the clearing.

Even at fourteen I was big enough to do some damage to Wyberg, and under different circumstances would have welcomed the opportunity to put a few well-placed bruises on Barbour's face, but the fight had drained out of me with the soul of the deer. They loaded both animals into Rich's dualie, backed over my mountain bike twice, and left me in the middle of the clearing soaked in a mixture of the deer's blood and my own.

I met Mr. Simet for the first time as his Humvee crested

a rise in the single-lane dirt road and swerved to miss me, walking directly down the middle toward town—"determination," as he put it, "smeared across my face in blood and dirt"—and he told me to get in. At first I wouldn't—couldn't—tell him what had happened. He stopped by his place to let me clean up and loan me some sweats so my mother wouldn't have to see me like that, but I took only a glass of water and asked to be taken home.

Simet said later he thought I was crazier than an outhouse rat, and he rendered a credible imitation of my ranting and raving the rest of the way to my house. "Rich Marshall had no right to kill either of those animals. That spoiled rich asshole isn't starving; he wasn't hunting food. His family owns an entire logging company, for Christ's sake. Rich Marshall hunts because he likes to hurt things. An entire football field isn't big enough to hold how big a shithead Rich Marshall is. I'm by God tired of living in a part of the country where you become a man by mounting some helpless animal's horns on the hood of the pickup your old man should have made you earn instead of dropping it on you like some Charlton Goddamn Heston rite-of-passage gift on your sixteenth birthday." Simet still re-creates that speech any time he catches me cranking up.

Other than telling me they were antlers, not horns, he let me purge, and when he dropped me off at my house, said I should probably call the cops; that if my story were even close to true, Rich Marshall should be prosecuted for assault.

No chance I was calling the cops, but the following Monday morning I pulled on my bloody T-shirt and jeans and, for the next five days, wore them to school like a soldier draped in his war-torn flag, telling everyone who asked and most who didn't where the blood came from and which unconscious ass wipe put it there—all in the face of significant opposition from the front office. In my imagination people would hear my story and demand that Rich Marshall have nothing further to do with Cutter High School; that even Wolverines Too would drop him like a smoking turd. Mr. Morgan requested that Mom and Dad intervene, citing a school rule prohibiting "disruptive attire"—a rule they used on me once when I wore a T-shirt with a cartoon depicting a proctologist standing over his patient, his dutiful nurse beside him, extending a can of beer. The caption read, "I said a butt light, not a Bud Lite." Actually, Mom and Dad sided with the school on that one.

But not this time. Morgan was, at the age of thirty-six, the youngest principal in school district history and lacked full appreciation of my parents' history growing up in the age of civil disobedience.

"Our son is disrupting his classes?" Dad asked as the three of us sat in Morgan's small inner office. I said before, Dad is a motorcycle guy, and he *looks* like a motorcycle guy: brown hair to his shoulders, an earring, tattoos gracing his massive forearms. He's real decent and articulate, but he looks like he eats children.

Morgan said, "In the sense that the bloody shirt attracts so much attention, yes."

"So the other students are refusing to work in order to stare at T. J.'s shirt? And the teachers are paralyzed from their duties because they can't take their eyes off him? Does that remain constant throughout the entire class period, or does it seem to dissipate when everyone gets bored with it?" Dad was never a fan of the controlling aspects of the educational system.

I think Morgan was beginning to sense that dealing with my parents might be more difficult than dealing with me. "Don't be absurd. That kind of behavior undermines the authority of the school in the students' eyes. Certainly as a parent you can understand that."

Dad said, "Don't take it on."

"Meaning?"

"Leave it alone. If you don't exercise authority over it, your authority won't be undermined." Then Dad asked if Morgan knew how my clothes got that way, and Morgan said there wasn't a hearing citizen in the county who didn't.

"And what are you doing about it?"

Morgan said it was outside school jurisdiction, a matter Dad and Mom could take up with the legal system if they so desired.

"Tell you what," Dad said, "we'll let it ride. And that should be a relief to you, because you've got this maniac running loose in your school and he's not even a student. T. J. knew what he was getting into when he went to the clearing; it's not as if Rich Marshall's reputation is a secret." Then he said, "Let me give you a piece of advice that could make your life easier. The last time I tried to power struggle this kid, he was five years old, and I was at least three years too late. I doubt you'll have any better luck than I did. If you suspend him, we'll support him however we have to. Truth is, I think this is a free-speech issue."

Mom was more succinct. "Suspend him and deal with our attorney."

Mr. Morgan was not one to welcome outside intervention, particularly of the legal variety, but he also didn't like being strong-armed with the culprit right there in the room. "What will you do if Rich takes matters into his own hands?"

40

I said, "He did that."

Mom said, "I'm assuming you have some control over an alumni group whose name is all over the printed programs for your football and basketball teams."

"Whose members you allow into your school building on a daily basis," Dad added.

"Of course, but that control is limited."

Dad said, "You make sure our son is safe during school hours and I'm sure he can take care of the rest. He's already survived the best Rich Marshall has to offer." He stood up, dwarfing Morgan. "We could have made a lot bigger fuss over this, sir. If I had a brain in my head, I'd get a restraining order that would put Rich Marshall three states away from my son. But T. J. talked me out of that. For now. If there's a *scent* of trouble, you will be getting some very bad publicity."

I wore my bloody garb of protest through the end of the week to no further administrative challenge. In the end I was proud to have forced Rich to take the head shot, spoiling the fawn as a trophy. There's always a pearl somewhere in the shit. Mom was proud she made the school think we had an attorney that wasn't her.

I can't look at Chris Coughlin without seeing myself. At one level that's strange; he's maybe five-eight and a hundred-thirty pounds, and before I got him swimming, five of those pounds were dirt. He can't have three percent body fat, and in a swimming suit you can see the outline of every tiny muscle in his body. He's pale as chicken gravy, and his eyes are dull as automobile primer. Only when he's tickled does a light flash behind them.

That could be me. When my bio-mom Glenda was at the top of her druggie game, she would leave me for days,

41

propped in the crib or the car seat, sucking on an empty bottle, crusted food on my chin and four-days-unwashed shirt. Strange men came in and out of her place at will. I've heard my mom say a thousand times that if you give her a drug-addicted mother with a kid under two, she'll give you a ninety-five percent chance of that kid getting molested or beat or both. I guess ninety-five kids had already gotten it, because I have no sense of that ever happening to me.

But the wrong guy, pissed at Glenda and whacked out on crank, could have changed the way my mind and body respond to the world in a heartbeat. So when I see a guy like Chris Coughlin eating shit, it's personal, and I mean in a bottom-level, core, DNA sense. Sometimes I trick myself into thinking I'm this righteous dude who stands up for the downtrodden, sort of a spiritual Robin Hood, an independent superhero who goes his own way, but the reality is, most of the time it's not a choice. Even though I have all these gifts, these physical and intellectual *treasures*, when I see someone getting kicked I *feel* it. Georgia, who was my childhood therapist, says it's because those first two years were full of losses, and even though I don't remember them in my mind, my body—my being—remembers.

So as this Far Side team assembles, I know I'm choosing an arbitrary battleground. Knee injuries aside, there is nothing inherently wrong with organized football or basketball, and there are guys who play and guys who coach who I have nothing but respect for. But sports here are too big a deal, the jocks get too much, and that doesn't leave enough for the rest of us. That wouldn't bother me as much except for the way Barbour and some of the real gung-ho guys use Chris and guys like him as examples of what happens to someone who wants a little piece of it, if only through the fading, worn letter jacket of his dead brother, as if they're delivering some *message* to the rest of us. I'd better be a little careful, or this could get too important.

A few days pass before I root out any more potential Aquamen—no Aquawomen are stepping up—but I do encounter a guy who will turn out to be integral to our swimming fortunes. Even before Simet strikes a deal for use of the pool at All Night Fitness, I start training on my own. Like I said, a lot of how you do in the last meet of the year depends on the number of miles you put in long before the first. I decide to swim late at night or early in the morning to avoid fifty-year-old ladies running laps up and down the lanes (what kind of workout is that?) and the Sidestroke Club, which is a group of ten or fifteen men and women who think they can get in shape swimming sidestroke about eight miles a day. I hate to tell them, but swimming sidestroke is the exercise equivalent of putt-putt golf.

I'm psyched to get going, and I wake up for my first workout at 2:30 A.M. All Night Fitness really is open all night, twenty-four hours a day, fifty-two weeks a year, Christmas included. I go overboard from the start, hitting the weight room first, alternating between upper body and legs, covering all the muscle groups; twelve reps on heavy weights, drop ten pounds for ten reps, drop ten more for eight. When my muscles feel like tapioca, I head for the pool, determined to flip my turns *only* at the shallow end so I can use that underwater shelf to knock myself silly enough to actually consider this project an intelligent undertaking. I'm not in good enough shape to hold my stroke for long distances, so I swim eighty-yard repeats leaving every minute-thirty seconds until there is an even chance the night guy will have to siphon me out of the scum gutter.

I've got to learn to start slower.

In the locker room I peel off my suit and stumble into the sauna. It's stone cold, so I flip the switch and sit naked on the cool redwood bench waiting for heat, breathing deep, feeling that sweet burn in my arms and chest.

A voice from nowhere. "You leave that on, you're gonna give me night sweats."

My yell ricochets off the walls like a bullet fired into a stainless-steel freezer. I see no one at first, then a foot slides out from under the bottom bench, followed by a leg, followed by a guy who turns out to be Oliver Van Zandt. He puts a finger to his lips. "Shut up or you'll bring in the night guy." He is dressed in gray sweatpants and a T-shirt, with a completely white beard and hair falling to his shoulders; looks like Gabby Hayes with muscles.

I say, "Man, you scared me to death."

"If I had, you'd make less noise."

"You fixing something under there?"

He opens the door, glances around the empty locker room, pulls it shut quickly. "I live here."

"In the sauna?"

"In the club," he says, and proceeds to detail a schedule that includes a full shift at Wendy's followed by one at Burger King. His son is a sophomore at U of W in Seattle. He can't afford a mortgage *and* tuition, so he joined All Night for just under thirty bucks a month, works out, showers and shaves here, and sleeps hidden out between the hours of eleven and four-thirty or so, when the place is virtually empty.

Man, this is hard to believe. "Do you always sleep in the sauna?"

"Never in the same spot two nights running," he says. "Sometimes I get into the pool equipment room, sometimes back in one of the exercise rooms under the mats. A moving target is hard to hit." He watches me carefully. "You gonna give me up?"

"You mean tell?"

"Yeah." His look is hard.

"Hell, no," I say. "Man, this is too good."

I flip off the heat switch to avoid overheating this guy's bedroom. You have to admit, living in a fitness spa has its allure; might not have exactly what you want in cushy furniture, but the weight machines provide about every kind of recliner you can think of, and you've got a bathroom with hair blowers on the wall and even a telephone. And a whirlpool. You'd pretty much have to stay at the Las Vegas Hilton for that.

I love the way life can put things in perspective for you. I'm worried about pulling it together enough to qualify for State in swimming while I put a little grief into Mike Barbour's life, and here's a guy who spends more than sixteen hours a day working for minimum wage with no benefits, who has given up his home so his son can escape the same fate. As I lie in my warm, comfortable bed, drifting off for a couple of hours before school, my quest seems less daunting.

4

Within the next two weeks we round out our swim team from the Sahara with guys cut from football and cross-country. (How do you get cut from cross-country?) I head over to the gym on both cut days, take down the names, spend a couple of days matching them with faces, then issue a personal invitation to those I believe would look most out of place in a Cutter High School letter jacket. Simet does his part by cementing a deal with All Night Fitness that allows us three hours workout time per day; one at 5:00 A.M. and the other two right after school. He stretches things a little, telling them I was once an Olympic hopeful, and that if I make it big, he'll make sure All Night gets good press.

"You told them I was an Olympic hopeful?"

"There must have been a time or two when you hoped you'd go to the Olympics someday," he says.

Ah, semantics.

"So how many more do you have for me?"

I say, "Drafted ten, landed three."

"Any that stand out?"

I smile. "Simon DeLong."

Simet flinches. "Simon DeLong weighs three hundred pounds."

"Two eighty-seven," I tell him. "And he's grown an inch. He's almost five-eight."

46

"How did you get him into a swimsuit?"

"I let him do that himself."

"Yeah, but how did he *find* one?"

"That was the easy part. I sent the Speedo people a body shot and told them he was determined to deck himself out in their stuff. Federal Express showed up a day later with swimsuits, warm-ups, goggles; all from Tyr. Shipped directly from Speedo headquarters."

Simet knows I'm lying but appreciates the humor. He shakes his head in true amazement. "God, what's it going to be to put Simon in a circle pattern?"

I say, "Dangerous."

"Who else?"

"Know a kid named Jackie Craig?"

Simet says he knows him by sight, but that's about it. Jackie is *non*descript. Medium build, brown hair, about five-ten; the kind of guy who could get away with robbing 7-11s because even if they caught him on camera, no characteristic would stand out. He's been cut from J.V. football.

"And last but not least?" Simet says.

"Andy Mott."

"Is that why you told me about Simon DeLong first?"

"You have to admit, never in the history of Cutter High School has a team of this diversity been assembled."

Simet considers, then, "I admit that."

If you look in the dictionary under surly, you'll find a picture of Andy Mott glaring back at you so hard the edges of the page will curl. He walks with a strange limp, though I don't know anyone who knows why. It isn't something you'd ask, and it isn't something he'd offer. He's a junior; a big guy, close to six-three. Tay-Roy says he benches major pounds and can do as many pull-ups as most guys can do sit-ups. In the hallway he limped up to me and said, "Heard you're looking for swimmers," and I said, "Yeah," and he said, "Sign me up," and it occurred to me that was eight more words than I'd ever heard him speak. I said, "Okay," already wondering what that would do to the long bus trips we were in for.

I start showing up at All Night around three-thirty every morning, knowing every mile I swim will pay off at the end of the season. Oliver Van Zandt says he'll pay me five bucks a week to find and wake him so he doesn't have to sleep with one eye open for the morning aerobics woman setting up for the early class, or some maintenance guy coming in early to make a pool repair.

He works out with me on weights, then watches me swim. It's nice to have the company.

At least things on my romantic horizons are calm through this, which I believed at one time would never be the case. I need that calm, rational, straightforward support in guiding this Bart Simpson swimming team through football city, and Carly Hudson gives it to me.

When my parents adopted me, they sent me to a child therapist because my two-year-old rage scared them. Her name is Georgia Brown and, simply put, she saved my life. I don't remember specifics, but she's quick to tell me I was a true hellion with an astonishing temper even by her standards, and she'd worked with kids like me almost ten years by then. In the face of the slightest frustration, I'd leap into the air, throw my legs straight out and land as hard as gravity would allow, or run, screaming, headlong into the side of the bathtub. If some other kid in my day care took a toy from me, or even had a toy I wanted, I went for that toy with malice aforethought, and all who resisted paid dearly. Mom and Dad took me to Georgia's playroom (in her home) once a week to work out the rage that accompanied the loss of my mother and the hours upon days of being left unattended.

Normally Georgia doesn't work with kids over five, but she either took a liking to me or didn't want my name on her list of future mass murderers, so though I don't see her formally now, when I feel the need I show up on her porch. She warned me back in junior high that I would have struggles with girls. "Lots of kids with your early childhood history have a real problem being left," she said. "The first girl you run into isn't likely to be the one for you, nor are you likely to be right for her. That will also be true of the second and the third. Which means what?" and before I could answer, "You're gonna get left, darlin'. Plenty of times. Get it through your peanut head."

Georgia gets away with calling my head peanut because she's mixed race, too. She's fond of saying if they called in an airstrike on the two of us having coffee, they would wipe out two-thirds of the people of color in town.

At any rate Georgia gave every warning I needed to avoid the landmines of love, and I proceeded to march into battle and step on every one. All the way through junior high and early high school, I picked girls flattered at how much I was willing to do for them. I carried their books, traded the best parts of my lunch for their sorry peanut butter sandwiches with no jelly, even did their homework. Each one loved it right up until she couldn't answer her doorbell without seeing my smiling face and started inventing reasons to ditch me, at which point I turned into a pint-sized stalker, walking by her house to see if she was home and who might be visiting her, calling and hanging up when she answered—all stuff that could get me arrested as an adult.

At the end of each crushing love affair I went to Georgia, and each time she told me, "Honey, you're always wantin' to make yourself indispensable. You figure if you help them with their worst problems, they'll never leave. Since you can't figure out exactly what their worst problems are, you help them with *all* their problems. Any girl who will let you do that is pretty sick. Healthy people want to solve their own problems, which, by the way, you have plenty of. Best way to be healthy in any relationship is to take care of yourself and let the other person do the same." She asked did I understand her.

I said I did, and to prove it I went right out and fell in love with Carly Hudson. I mean facedown in the soup in love; head-banging, eye-popping, short-of-breath, plead-with-the-universe-till-your-voice-box-is-raw kind of love. The kind of love so deep that, when it's not going the way you want it to, your *ancestors* moan. She's a jock, which appeals to me out of the chute. Dark hair, dark eyes, makeup applied with a subtle artist's eye and hand. There is no butt-twitching or flirtatious glancing or any of the symptoms that usually rocket me to Hormone City, but her natural sexuality is jarring.

I'm one of those guys who's loquacious in love. Our first real date was for a Coke on a study break, and by the time it was over, I had already told her she took my breath away. She was quiet a few minutes, then proceeded to say that was the fastest way she could think of to get her to change her phone number. If Georgia had been going to pick one girl out of the billions inhabiting the planet, this is the one she would have picked, the one least likely to *ever* let me fix her life.

I met her on the river. It was the end of summer between my sophomore and junior years, one of those dry, hot days when everyone is at the river the minute they finish whatever they had to do for the day, which for most of us is before ten o'clock in the morning. That was the summer I'd decided to become a championship water skier and wake-boarder. I'd get up at four in the morning as the sun peeked over the mountains to the east, pick up a couple of buddies, get the boat on the water while it was smooth as an ice-skating rink, and ski until the winds came up, then hang out on the dock or the beach until evening when the water calmed again to the point that you could see the reflection of the mountains as clearly as you could see the mountains themselves, and ski or wake-board until dark. I was in my Speedo about eighteen hours a day.

Carly was new that year. Her dad is this big-time builder from over in northern Idaho and had contracted to build a fancy resort hotel on the river, then develop a couple of high-rent subdivisions. Between all the new high-tech industries and resort developments, Cutter is one of the faster-growing towns in the state. At any rate, I was pretty popular that summer because of the boat, and for the price of a few gallons of gas I'd take almost anyone for a spin on the skis. In return, they had to drive while I skied. I was working my way through this makeshift slalom course a few of us had rigged up when I spotted Carly and a couple of girls from my class walking onto the city dock, and I signaled Mike Morrow to take me in. I glided toward the dock, turned around as I reached it and sat, perfectly dry above the knees, very cool.

Carly walked over, failed to mention my studly landing, but struck up a conversation. Before I knew it, I was showing her the sights up where the river narrows, in the wilder, faster water. I pulled close to shore, out of the current near water that swirled deep beneath shady pine trees. I can't even remember what we talked about, but all of a sudden two hours were gone and I was pretty much thunderstruck.

I was cool, didn't ask her to the Legion Hall dance that night, figuring she'd show up with friends and I'd nab her away. Only the friend she showed up with was Mike Barbour. The deer incident, my cultural heritage, and the fact that I wouldn't turn out for sports had already locked Barbour and me into Christian-gladiator status.

Barbour has always been popular in that loud, conquering-hero sort of way. Since middle school he was ahead of his time: first guy to shave, first to throw back a six-pack. On the dance floor he showed pelvic action worthy of Elvis. Carly kept him at a distance, but it was killing me that she walked in with him, or that she danced with him at all. Old stirrings of not being chosen welled up, and my first instinct was to get out of there because that particular feeling has historically resulted in bad behavior. On the other hand, I was majorly pissed at myself for not asking her to the dance earlier; the window that had opened seemed about to close and lock. So when Barbour went to take a leak, I asked her to dance. She smiled and said she *thought* that was me standing over there by myself.

I thought, Right. In the middle of a part of the United States so white that every fourth year some group of survivalist assholes formally petitions Congress to create a fifty-first state from the land between here and Missoula, Montana, for whites only, she *thinks* she sees the same Kung Fu Jackie Robinson she spent two hours on the river with this afternoon. I didn't have the words for that, so I said, "Yeah, I'm hard to miss. How do you ladies do it?"

"What?"

"You've been in town two days and already found the biggest asshole we've got."

She smiled. "Guess he reminds me of my father."

"Is that good or bad?" I was being haunted by the feeling that goes with the knowledge that something you really want is going to the very worst possible place. God, where in the rule book does it say that the good guy, the guy that's easy to talk to, the guy who unties the damsel from the railroad tracks seconds before the train would cut her into thirds, gets to be the *friend*, while the asshole gets the good stuff? That's how my mind gets going when I expect the worst.

"It's bad. But I always have to check those guys out. You know, to be sure of my instincts."

Instant relief. I don't totally understand it. Some people will have asshole parents and turn out just like them, like Barbour or Rich Marshall. Others see through it and turn out the opposite. I discovered later that night Carly hadn't had it easy. Ol' man Hudson's a hard-drinking hardass who's never satisfied, and he used to knock his wife around in a minute if she got out of line. When Carly was a freshman, back in Idaho, her dad talked her into turning out for the J.V. cheerleading squad instead of basketball and volleyball because he thought being a jock was "unfeminine." "I hated the idea, but I was a cutie," she told me. "When the student votes were in, I had more than there were students. And remember I said Dad talked me into it."

As I found out later, when Carly's involved with something, she's gotta have her hands on every part of it, so she helped design the outfits, worked up new yells, and even choreographed some dances. At halftime of the first J.V.

basketball game the cheerleaders joined the drill team in a song-and-dance thing Carly had worked up. The grand finale required the three cheerleaders to bend over and flip up their skirts so people could read THS. The small crowd cheered wildly, even the players pointed and clapped, and old man Hudson came out of the bleachers like he was nuclear powered, grabbed Carly by the elbow, and jerked her toward the door, screaming that she was a whore and a bitch, and the next time he caught her showing her ass he'd beat her half to death.

"The crowd sat stunned until we were out the door. A couple of other parents told me later they tried to follow, but by the time they recovered from their shock, we were driving out of the parking lot. That night I got a beer opener from the kitchen and a ball peen hammer from the garage and redecorated his brand-new Lexus; smashed all the glass and ran the beer opener down each side, fender to fender. Then I went back into the house, threw my tools of destruction at his feet, and told him for every mark he put on me or my mom, I'd put another one on the car, and if he wanted to start right now, go right ahead, but be prepared to explain himself to the newspaper and the TV station."

I said, "Whoa!"

"Yeah, whoa," she said back. "He was a well-respected businessman who didn't need the bad press. He hasn't laid a hand on me or my mother since. The next day I turned my cheerleader's uniform in to the office and asked if I could try out late for basketball."

Of course there are scars. Carly is a talent in a lot more areas than just sports. She can sing, I swear she has a photo-graphic memory, plus she's fashion-model good-looking in the face, though way too strong and powerful to be consid-

54

ered anywhere near that in the body. Yet, when I asked her once what she thought she was very best at, she said, "Packing."

I said, "Packing? Packing what?"

She said, "Clothes, hair dryer, makeup, food. Before our nonviolence treaty I could pack everything my mother, little brother, and I would need for three days, in just under the time it took my dad to run to Zip Trip for another half-rack of beer after he loosened my mother's teeth." She went on to tell me how she'd drag her and her brother's suitcases over four-foot snowdrifts, staying off the road, because her dad would find them gone, grab a couple of beers, and patrol the streets.

Jesus. "Why three days?"

"Because that's the longest my mother ever stayed away." She said she probably disliked her mother more than her dad, because she hated the weakness she saw every time her mother went crawling back. "I'd have been out of there a long time ago if it weren't for my brother," she said. "I gave up on Mom by the time I was twelve. Thomas is turning sixteen this year and he's almost as big as Dad, so I don't think there'll be any trouble."

Then, in answer to the unasked question of why she was telling me all this, she said, "So here's the deal with me and guys, bubba. If we're friends, we're friends. If we have sex, we have sex. I don't sleep with more than one person, and I won't go with anyone who does. We double up on birth control. And *no*body runs my life, which means I don't go in for a bunch of whining when I have something important to do and you want to go to the prom. You interested?"

Actually, at that point I was still stuck back where she said, "If we have sex, we have sex."

55

I was interested, and the rest is history. Georgia Brown says Carly saved me from having to learn that middle-school lesson over and over again into my fifties.

Funny how everything is relative. If *my* father were ever to behave the way Mr. Hudson behaves, he'd spend the rest of his life begging forgiveness—from the Turkish prison my mother would see to it he was sentenced to. And if anyone ever broke my mother's jaw, they'd better be ready to take a bullet.

So if I'm Carly, a good day is one in which no one in my family gets brutalized; and if I'm Chris Coughlin, a good day is when nobody calls me dummy and the football players don't jack me up, and somebody puts their hand on my shoulder and smiles at me when they see me staring at my dead brother's picture in the trophy case. If I'm The Tao Jones, a good day is when I lock onto whatever I'm passionate about and pursue it with abandon, whether it's swimming, or messing with Mike Barbour's head, or a good journalism story, or Carly Hudson.

If you're my father, a good day is one in which you avoid remembering the events of July 27, 1968.

Everything is relative.

5

Our family legacy of helping kids runs deep. The more obvious source would be my mother, working as she does in the juvenile court division of the attorney general's office on child-abuse cases. Plus, she was the one so quick to snap up my raggedy two-year-old butt when my bio-mom called it quits. But the kid thing goes back further, into a darker hole.

My dad was one of those smart guys who doesn't do squat in school. He never forgets *anything* he's interested in, and he can assemble almost any gadget without instructions. When we get some new electronic gizmo, like a VCR or a digital camera or a scanner to go with the computer, he doesn't even take the instructions out of the little plastic envelope. He says the guys who write those things start by telling you not to stand in the bathtub when you plug it in; that you'll read three-quarters of the booklet before running into your first piece of useful information. I'll bet his I.Q. is someplace in the one-sixties, but when I asked him once what he remembered most about high school, he said, "The clock."

So, due more to attention span than ability, he skipped college and went to work in a Harley shop out of high school, then enrolled in truck-driving school on his twenty-first birthday, thinking he'd get paid the big bucks to see

57

the country. What he got paid to see, again and again and again from the cab of his ten-wheeler, was the country between Boise, Idaho, and a small town called New Meadows, a hundred-fifty miles north on winding two-lane. He got to be a small-time hero in that town, hauling meat and produce and bread and beer and information from the capital city; everyone knew his truck when it rolled into town, and everyone waved.

One day, after he'd been driving the route about a year, he stayed for lunch with a young widow who worked at the New Meadows Merc, which is like a general store, and whose husband had been killed in a hunting accident two years earlier. Big and scary looking as he can be on first sight, that's how gentle and understanding my dad is when you get to know him. As Dad tells it, the widow was just beginning to come out of the shell she'd created around herself following her husband's death. Her baby was eighteen months old, had never known his father. The widow's mother took care of the baby while they had lunch at the exclusive Pine Knot Cafe, and they both felt some chemistry bubbling. She took him to her house, where they made fast, hot, electric love, uncharacteristic for either of them, to hear Dad tell it.

When Dad got the widow back to the store, he was behind schedule, so he jumped into his truck, confident traffic would be light that time of afternoon, that he had a pretty good chance of making up most of the time he'd lost. The lovemaking had transported him; it was the sweetest he'd felt in years.

But somehow while the baby's grandmother wasn't looking, the little boy had crawled under the truck and got caught between the rear dual tires. It was several minutes before anyone realized the baby was missing, and they quickly searched the store, hitting the obvious places before the widow was struck with the unthinkable and jumped into her car to chase after Dad, hoping beyond rationality that the baby had somehow gotten into the trailer. She discovered a small severed arm lying next to the white line about a mile and a half outside the city limits, maybe a hundred yards from where the truck spit out the rest of the little boy's mangled body.

The state patrol let Dad get home before telling him, in hopes there would be a family member or a boss to help him with the emotional sledgehammer that was about to thunder into his chest, so it was almost six hours after the baby's death that Dad discovered what he'd done.

I was twelve when he told me that story, in response to my kidding him about whether or not he'd ever had a real job. He'd always known he'd tell me someday, because it became the defining moment in his life. For years, it was *who he was*. I don't know that I was ready to hear it; I woke up with nightmares every night for two weeks, but I haven't seen him the same since.

"I thought I'd have to kill myself," he told me later, "just to end the pain. For more than two years it was constant; didn't ease up when I worked out, when I slept, when I rode my bike a hundred miles an hour, or when I used drugs, and believe me, buddy, I used them all. Nothing touched it. I literally ached for the relief of being gone. The law wouldn't charge me, the widow wouldn't sue me for every penny I would ever make; I can't tell you how bad I needed to be punished, but no one would do it.

"I took a job in a sawmill in a small logging town on my old route, worked a full forty-hour shift every week, then

59

volunteered to sub for anyone calling in sick. I'd keep enough of my paycheck for rent and food and send the rest to the widow, but after a couple of months it started coming back. There was simply no way to get redemption."

Dad always called the woman "the widow," though I know he knows her name. He said he couldn't bring himself to say it. "I sometimes consider those six hours," he said, "when the deed was done, but I didn't know it yet. Driving back toward Boise, letting my mind wander back over our slow lunch, the light in her eyes, her soft hair; I considered they might be the best six hours of my life. She was so . . . elegant. When she reached across the table in the Pine Knot and touched my hand, we both knew what would happen next. And yet, in those same six hours, when I was on top of the world, the world had already crumbled under me. I was riding back toward Boise on the cloud of a lie."

Dad's fifty-three now; that happened more than thirty years ago, and though he's done whatever he needed to do to accommodate that astonishing incident into his life, I believe no day goes by that it doesn't touch him in some way. My father will not have a mousetrap in the house; he slides a card or a piece of paper under a spider or potato bug to deposit it safely outside, rather than step on it. He won't say it, but Mom thinks he believes the only way to buy his way out of hell is to protect every life that comes into his sphere of influence. Scary looking as he is, children flock around my father as if he were created by Walt Disney. He is the most patient man I know; it is a patience born of agony.

Dad doesn't have that part of the male ego that gets edgy if your wife makes more money than you do. Mom makes a darned good living. Dad makes squat. What income he does have comes from restoring classic motorcycles, or making repairs in his garage at home. Everything else he does free. He's a Guardian ad Litem, which is a volunteer through juvenile court to represent children in child-abuse cases. The state can't afford to pay real attorneys to represent children's best interests in court, so they train volunteers. It requires that he get to know the kids on his caseload, as well as their parents, and work with therapists and case-workers to help reunite the kids with their parents, or get them out of there if it appears the parents can't pull it off. He also volunteers his "play" services at a couple of day cares and works with the local Head Start coordinating play activities a couple of times a week. He could turn some of those things into paying jobs, but he told himself after the accident that he would never do anything for children for his own financial gain. I think it's also the reason he doesn't discipline me much. That comes from my mother. Because of Dad, I don't even have a curfew.

It's funny. Dad doesn't attend church, and it is seldom I hear his spiritual take on anything. But the running over of that little boy almost turned him into a saint, as far as his public behavior goes. He still has his temper, and there are times when you just steer clear of him simply in response to the look in his eye, but I don't know a human being in the world more determined to do "right." Sometimes I wonder how much effect that event has had on *me*, how it might have been one of those awful trade-offs in which I got a lot more of my father's attention through his quest for redemption.

Things start falling into place with the swim team. Unfortunately things also start falling into the water. All the

61

guys but Andy Mott begin showing for the morning workout. All Night provides each of us a temporary free membership entitling use of the entire facility in return for
placing a small logo on our tank suits and another on the
chest of our warm-ups. So I guess you could call us the Cutter All Night Wolverines.

But big-time organization is in order. The narrow lanes
do *not* accommodate circle patterns. For one thing, Simon
DeLong's particular body design barely allows for all of *him*
in one lane, much less another person. It is increasingly
clear that, while he may never be very fast, he'll always
start at an advantage off the dive when the competitors on
either side grab on to the lane ropes to keep from being
washed into the gutter. Unfortunately, during workouts,
we play the parts of those competitors. Chris and Dan Hole
are small enough to swim in one lane, but Chris's mind
tends to wander and it doesn't come back until he's had a
header with Dan, who then stops to explain to him, in
terms Chris couldn't possibly understand, the theory
behind circle patterns. Hell, I *know* the theory and don't
understand Dan's explanation.

Tay-Roy and I tried to share a lane, but we both have
shoulders like I-beams, and though we can pass each other
nine times out of ten without incident, one of us will get
hurt on that tenth time. The point is, swimming is supposed to be a noncontact sport and the All Night Wolverines are about to end up spending the lion's share of our per
diem on aquatic bicycle helmets.

Both Dad and Georgia say over and over that the universe offers up whatever we need whenever we need it. I
think the universe offers up way more than we need most
of the time, but they may have a point. One morning about

quarter after four I'm sitting on the toilet at home, unloading the extra cargo before taking to the water, and I solve our space problem. Rain the night before has brought three or four little black potato bugs up through the drain and into the bathtub; the kind of bugs I said my dad scoops up and takes outside. When they get caught in the tub like that, without human intervention they're doomed, because once they crawl to the curve of the tub they become like barefoot children trying to climb a glacier. If you're Dad, that's when you scoop them up, but it occurs to me that our bathtub is All Night Fitness for potato bugs. These babies have to be getting into peak shape, like the thong-leotard ladies on the treadmills at the real All Night, only nowhere near as easy to watch.

So between workout and school, I stop by Delaney's Hardware and pick up some industrial strength I-bolts, get permission from the owner of All Night to secure them into the wall, hook plastic handles to surgical tubing, and run them through the I-bolts. So when four of us are swimming, the other three can lie on their stomachs on a wooden bench placed back far enough to get proper tension on the surgical tubing and swim in place. All Night has already granted us permission to crank up a boom box, so what could be an astonishingly tedious workout turns into a form of on-your-belly rock-and-roll dancing. It is getting us in great shape, though I'm pretty sure we don't look much smarter than potato bugs. An aerial view of this would have to be ugly.

The other guys want to keep me in the water most of the time because if we are to score points, I'll be getting most of them, but I won't take more water time because I can rack up distance during off hours, and at this point camaraderie is as important as miles. I mean, we are going to have to like each other a *lot* to get through the season, and we are not exactly computer matched for personality compatibility.

One unexpected gain. Loud music at four-thirty is not conducive to sleep, so Oliver Van Zandt has become our unofficial interim coach until Simet can come on board, just after Thanksgiving, according to state regulations. Oliver knows squat about swimming, but he's been an athlete all his life, so he studies the workout Simet and I prepare, and yells at us the entire time. This is truly becoming a Far Side swimming team.

I phone Simet late one afternoon after workout. "You need to take me to dinner."

"Why can't we just meet in my room after school, or during your study hall?"

"Because the best I could get there is that wretched fried egg sandwich your wife sends with you. Why don't you tell her how cold and hard that thing gets?"

We meet at a little Italian place he likes, which I'm sure he thought would intimidate me because the menu is hard to read and most of the diners dress relatively well. Guess again. My father and I have a common tie, and I can turn it and a shirt and a pair of Dockers into a *G.Q.* thing for sure.

Simet orders a glass of wine and a Coke for me. "So why are you plaguing me? And whatever happened to pizza?"

"Pseudo-Italian," I tell him. "It doesn't cost enough."

He reaches over and grips my triceps. "You getting into shape?"

"Against all odds," I say. "Getting in five to six thousand yards."

"Are the other guys showing up?"

I assure him they are. "I'm working some with Chris;

getting him used to the idea of being on a team and getting on a schedule. I'm worried about what he'll do the first time he hears a starter gun."

"What about DeLong and Mott?"

"Haven't seen Mott yet." I don't tell him it's to my relief. You never know what Mott is thinking, whether he's simply feeling ornery—a natural state for him—or if he's plotting a mass murder. "Simon's there like clockwork." I shake my head in wonder. "He's the only guy I've ever seen who can raise the water level in a swimming pool." I take a long drink. "We still need to talk about letter requirements."

"I told you not to worry, you'll get your letter."

"Yeah, but I'm thinking about the other guys."

Simet says, "We can make it a particular number of points. A first place gets you five. Second is three and third is one. You can swim three individual events or two individuals and a relay. Let's say you earn a letter if you average two points per meet."

I consider our personnel. Most of them won't beat anyone on the other team and will only pick up third-place points in the events I'm not swimming or in events where the other team swims only one swimmer. I say, "How about just if they don't drown?"

Simet laughs. "Somewhere between lies a compromise. We've got time to think about it. We have to be careful; the athletic department has a lot of pride at this school, and a lot of clout. The letter jacket is the ultimate prize. I'm going to have to be judicious if I want respect in the coaching fraternity." He is only half joking.

"Well," I say, "somehow we have to put it within reach."

* * *

There is something seriously messed up about Rich Marshall being around as much as he is. Since he's now the head guy at Marshall Logging, he seems able to take off as much time as he wants to play school, which he's been doing to some degree since the year after he graduated. I mean, the guy never left, was roaming the halls back when I was a freshman. I understand why the football coaches want him around; he was a real monster when he played, and he's a good guy to introduce psychopathy to the other players. But he also volunteers in PE classes sometimes, which puts him in the halls during the regular school day way more than I'd like. He's kind of a cross between a kid and an adult, and I mean that in the least flattering terms of either. You see him in the coaches' room being treated like an assistant, but you also see him hanging out between classes with Barbour and the more arrogant members of the football team. A couple of times I've caught him staring at me with the same look he had when I wore my bloody T-shirt to school, and he makes continual references to the fact that they could sure use me out there on the football field, *if I had the heart for it.* He also remarked recently on the number of black guys in the swimming hall of fame. Because of the deer incident my freshman year, my parents have offered to raise hell that he's there at all, but I don't want that. Hey, when he's here, at least I know where he is.

And now he's popping up in even more corners of my life. I stop by Georgia Brown's house after workout a few days after my conversation with Simet about the letter jackets, just to see what's going on. She doesn't answer the door, but I have walk-in privileges, so I snatch some Gatorade out of the fridge, turn on Sports Center, and make myself comfortable on the couch. Within seconds, big commotion spills down from upstairs, which tells me Georgia's in the thick of a therapy session, and I sneak a few steps up to see if I can get a glimpse into the playroom. Georgia sees me through the stair railing and motions me on up.

Play therapy, as practiced by Georgia Brown, is done live and full scale, meaning she will drag in anybody available to play the roles that allow the kids to work out their life traumas. Most times I'm a bad dad they want to tie up and put in prison, so my job is to struggle and struggle and never get loose while still protecting my nuts. As I said before, I've been on the other end of this, so I never refuse.

Inside the playroom a girl of about four or five, with almost my exact coloring, plays with dolls. Georgia whispers, "This is Heidi. Think we're gonna need a bad dad here."

Heidi has dragged a plastic basket full of dolls to the middle of the room, where she sorts them by color, placing the fair-skinned ones into cradles, tucking them in tenderly, singing bits of lullabies. The darker-skinned dolls don't fare so well; flung across the room, stuffed behind toy appliances, some beheaded or otherwise dismembered. She looks up.

"This is T. J.," Georgia says to her. Heidi looks at me, *through* me, and turns her attention back to the white dolls. She sings, urges Georgia to do the same. Occasionally she glances at me but quickly turns away, gives the dolls bottles, nurtures them like a nurse.

Suddenly she stands and marches right to me, grabbing my hand. She says, "You be the bad dad." I've played it frequently, know the role. Interesting that the kids all use the same term.

I say, "Okay, I'm the bad dad."

"Find all the nigger dolls," she says.

Georgia nods.

"You mean the dark-colored ones?"

"The *nigger* dolls!" she screams at me.

Georgia nods again.

I say, "The nigger dolls." I retrieve two.

"Scream," Heidi orders.

"What should I scream?"

"Stupid black bitch!"

"What?"

"Stupid bitch!" she yells again. "Black bitch!"

Again Georgia nods. I don't like this particular bad dad role.

I look at a doll, raise my voice, and call it a stupid black bitch.

"Me!" Heidi screams. "Yell it at *me!*" She turns to Georgia. "Make him do it right!"

In a calm voice Georgia tells me I'm supposed to yell at Heidi for letting the black dolls in the house, and I finally piece together from Heidi that I'm also supposed to find them one by one, scream at Heidi for letting each one in ("Get these nigger babies out the house! They stinky!"), and throw them out, and it wouldn't hurt if I kicked or punched them while I'm at it. It's a lot easier to hear that word than to say it to a little kid, because I know the impact when you aren't steeled against it. But Georgia knows what she's doing.

As I get deeper into my role, Heidi turns back to the white babies, tucking them tighter, rocking them as she rocks herself, never engaging me unless I lose zeal for my task.

I find the last doll crammed inside an igloo dog house

Georgia has turned into a cave for some other kid and jerk it out by the arm, open the door to the hallway, and fling it, only to see someone disappearing down the stairs. I am caught for one moment in mid-scream, but Heidi screams, "GET THESE GODDAMN FUCK NIGGER KIDS OUT THE HOUSE!!!" and the dead come alive and I am back in business. I hear the front door slam.

Minutes later in the living room, Georgia touches my shoulder. "You okay, baby?" Since I was two she's called me baby.

"Yeah, I'm okay." I nod toward the kitchen, where Heidi plays. "I can think of better things than nigger to holler at a kid."

"Over and over I tell you, racism is—"

"Ignorance," I say back.

The sound of running water brings our attention to Heidi in the kitchen, squeezing dish soap into the filling basin. She pulls herself up onto the lip, stretching to snag a bristle brush, then begins scrubbing her arms. Georgia sighs, closes her eyes, whispers, "She thinks if she can wash it off, her daddy will love her."

Heidi's eyes focus on her brown arms, scrubbing. Georgia moves to the sink and kneels beside her, draping her arms over the lip next to Heidi's. Heidi stops scrubbing. Georgia says, "Hey." Heidi doesn't answer, but glances down at Georgia's arms, then runs her fingers softly over Georgia's forearm.

Georgia motions me over and I take the clue, kneeling on the other side of Heidi, soaping up my arm.

She looks sadly into my eyes. "You're a dirty nigger, too."

Georgia's look tells me this is not a time for political correctness. "Yeah, I guess so."

Heidi's sudsy hand touches my face. She looks sorry for me.

I take the brush, begin scrubbing my own arm. "Dang," I tell her. "I don't think it comes off."

She says, "Wait," and pulls herself again over the lip of the sink, stretches to grab a soap bar, then squirts the liquid soap over it and hands it to me. She says, "Two soaps." I wash my arm like crazy, then rinse. We both stare at my arm. "Nope," I say, "what else can we try?" Georgia backs away, and for the next few minutes Heidi and I try every kind of brush-soap combination she can imagine, including turning the water in the basin cold.

Finally I say, "Know what?"

"What?"

"I think we're stuck with it."

Heidi takes a long last look at my arm, then walks me to the hand towel hanging from the refrigerator handle. I dry my arm and she does the same.

My forearm is red and raw on the spot where we've been performing our ethnic cleansing experiment. I say, "Know what else?"

"What?"

"If we keep this up, we could hurt ourselves."

Minutes later, Heidi on my shoulders, I two-step around the living room to a Bob Marley CD I have convinced her is the hottest thing since Barney. There is nothing of the rage and desperation of the last two hours in her eyes, but I'm aware of Georgia's continuous assertion that the only pure evil is nothing. For this moment, high atop my shoulders, Heidi squeals, visible and proud. But I know she'll come crashing down the moment she is degraded again. I know—just because I know—that despair moves in like a flash flood when she is diminished. It isn't even about race, really. It's about nothingness.

Georgia emerges from her office with a form and a pen, lifts Heidi off my shoulders, hands me the form, and says, "Sign this."

"What is it?"

"A confidentiality oath."

"What?"

"It's a signed statement that you won't tell anyone anything that goes on here in therapy," she says. "So I can have you work with Heidi, or any other kid who needs you when you're around."

"You're hiring me?"

She laughs. "For *far* under minimum wage. I'm keeping my license safe, baby."

I glance at the written oath, dated two weeks ago. "This is old."

"Predated," she says back. "Sign it before Heidi's mother gets here. She's already seen you with her."

I don't get it.

"Didn't I see Alicia in the hall when you threw the doll out?"

"Alicia *Marshall?*" *Click!* I look at Heidi. "Alicia Marshall's your mom?"

She looks away.

"This is Rich Marshall's kid? He did this?"

"Watch your tone," Georgia says. "You're a professional."

I start to answer, but Georgia glances at Heidi and quickly back at me with a look that says *later*.

71

I disappear into the kitchen when Alicia returns, after which Georgia extracts two of the finest homemade oatmeal cookies currently in production from her cookie jar. "Here," she says, "You deserve these."

"I'm getting paid in cookies?"

"Get used to it."

"Jesus, I knew Alicia had a mixed-race kid, but it didn't even *occur* to me that was her."

"You know a lot of mixed-race kids in this town? Guess I better bring you up to speed, darlin'."

I know part of this story already, but now Georgia fills me in on the rest. When he graduated from high school against all odds, notorious deer-slayer Rich Marshall went to work in the woods setting chokers for his dad's logging company, passing up the chance to play football at the local community college long enough to bring his grades up to an even 0.00 so he could attend an NCAA Division I school. His girlfriend, Alicia Dalton, signed up at the beauticians' school at Spokane River Community College, dumped Rich, began dating a black defensive back named Willis Stack, and got pregnant.

I won't go into the white supremist militia dogma Rich began spouting in response to "this interracial travesty in our midst," but Alicia was in love, and she and Willis decided to get married. Then Willis was paralyzed from the neck down as a result of a crushing hit he laid on a wide receiver from Wenatchee. The story goes he couldn't bear to think of raising his kid in that condition or of saddling Alicia with his care, so in the middle of the night, about three weeks after he was released from the hospital, his brothers loaded him into their van and spirited him away, leaving Alicia heartbroken and lost. She dropped out of school, had the baby—which she named after Willis's sister

Felicia—and went to work as a checker at Jensen Brothers Foods, where good old Rich shopped for his frozen TV dinners and Chee-tos and Budweiser and started courting her again, every bit as pissed off as he was the day she started dating Willis.

In her defeated state, Alicia believed Rich when he said nobody would have her "nigger baby" but him, and they entered into wedded bliss, legally changed Felicia's name to Heidi because it was the "whitest" name Rich could think of, became parents to twin boys nine months to the day from the wedding, and settled into a life of what Alicia described to Georgia as hell on earth. That gives hell *and* earth a bad rap in my book. Heidi was not allowed to touch food other family members might eat, or play with her younger brothers' toys except on special occasions, which occurred when Rich said they occurred, or when he was out of town or passed out on the couch. This guy was every girl's parents' nightmare, a control freak with an I.Q. three points lower than his belt size.

Child Protection Services got involved through an anonymous report when Rich decided Heidi had earned twenty-five "spanks" with his belt—ten for forgetting to clean her room, five for dropping her dessert on the floor after he'd told her to be careful, and ten for not washing out the dog's bowl—and demanded that Alicia deliver the blows to his specifications. When Alicia turned out not to have the heart for it, Rich took over and Heidi was black and blue from the middle of her back to her knees. Rich's parents got him an attorney who was able to plea-bargain him down from an assault charge, and the kids were placed out of the home until Rich learned to manage his rage and meanness and Alicia learned to protect them from his rage and meanness.

73

Now this is where I don't get it about males and females in so-called civilized America. Alicia Marshall is a good-looking woman, and she's smart enough that she sure didn't have to settle for whatever emerged from the nearest manhole. She told Georgia she *loved* Willis Stack, and Georgia says it's clear she loves Heidi. What could be inside a person that could allow an asshole like Rich Marshall to come along and take her kid apart? Georgia says it's what *isn't* inside a person.

At any rate, they both started into mental-health treatment, but Rich blew out of it in the first week. Anger management group and parenting classes got in the way of his drinking beer, a problem he solved by giving up the classes. Alicia got the kids back with the promise that she would stay in treatment and would never see Rich in their presence. That was perfect for Rich because he didn't like the kids all that much anyway, and he could see her often enough to make sure she knew she'd never learn to live without him. In my view, learning to live without Rich Marshall is like learning to live without cholera, but nobody asked me.

As I walk toward my car from Georgia's house, what I know is this: The feeling I had inside when Heidi and I were scrubbing ourselves "clean" will keep Rich Marshall in my life long after I would normally have had him surgically removed like a giant hemorrhoid. No way can I turn away from Heidi now; her sorrow for my color has to be repaired. I'm big enough—old enough—to stop guys like Rich, but Heidi's not. Georgia's right about bigotry: that absent the element of hate, a person's skin color is only an indication of his or her geographical ancestry. But *with* that element, it is a soul stealer.

6

Time passes, and the swim team gets better and better, not in the sense that we're ever going to win a meet, or even a race that I'm not in, but in the sense that no one is turning back.

Tay-Roy is turning into our go-to butterflyer. He operates on power and endurance, and big as those shoulders are, they are amazingly flexible. He doesn't yet have the stroke timing right, but he's down and back in the time it takes any of the others to get down. That alone won't win races, but it will avoid crippling embarrassment.

Chris Coughlin is so glad to be a part of something he works like one of those potato bugs in my bathtub, and he's as happy stroking away belly down on the bench as he is in the water. In fact, he likes it more because he can hear the music better. We've been democratic about music selection, and Chris likes Christmas music, so interspersed with all the rock and hard-driving country and rap (and Dan Hole's "1812 Overture") comes "Rudolf the Red-Nosed Reindeer." Chris likes the Gene Autry version.

Water is the very best place for Dan Hole because he can't talk when his face is in it, and the longer he's quiet the more likable he becomes. Simon has realized he doesn't weigh close to three hundred pounds in the water, and after the first two weeks of working out and lifting weights,

Interim Coach Oliver thought he saw the outline of triceps poking through the meat. I caught Simon later in the locker room when he thought everyone was gone, straightening his arm to flex, smiling and shaking his head. A boy and his muscle.

Interim Coach Oliver, the permanent uninvited houseguest of All Night, is an entity unto himself. As I said, he knows nothing about swimming, but he's a master motivator and is a better influence the more screwed up the athlete is. Having brought Simon to playing with the idea that there's a Tay-Roy Kibble inside him ready to burst through at any time, he's focused his energy on converting Dan into a "regular guy who's able to converse with his peers," demanding ten push-ups every time he uses a word Oliver doesn't understand. It's too early to tell, but I think Dan has a better chance of building his pecs to Schwarzeneggerian bulk than dumbing down his vocabulary for the likes of us. The guy even *bitches* in high-brow: "I'm punished for bringing aristocratic flair to the language and vocabulary of these aquatic Cro-Magnons?" he says. "How can that be?"

Interim Coach Oliver belches and says, "You're damn lucky I know 'aristocratic.' I ain't so sure which ones were the Cro-Magnons. Gimme ten more."

Interim Coach Oliver created a "station" system, wherein one station is the pool, one the surgical-tubing-bench-humping swimming, one a series of deck drills—jumping jacks to push-ups to sit-ups to dips. Three minutes all-out in each station, three times around, to the sound of Interim Coach Oliver's booming voice, gets us going pretty good when we're bored with the tedium of the long workouts. Three days a week we hit the weight room, where Tay-Roy puts us through a killer weight workout he dreamed up after reading how Olympic swimmers weight train.

Don't get me wrong. In the long run a swimmer is the product of, more than anything else, the number of yards he or she can log in the water. We're feeling good on the front end of all this, but when the season starts we'd better have some creative individual goals, because we're going to get our asses kicked. If I have my way, though, when the season is over, there will be six guys stalking the halls you couldn't have *imagined* wearing the holy shroud of blue and gold.

Things are less optimistic out in "real" life. Alicia Marshall must have told Rich she saw me in Heidi's play-therapy session because every time I ran into him at school the next day, he squinted one eye as if he was lining me up in the crosshairs, then turned away. He doesn't know I get power knowing he knows I have the goods on him. He's a guy to watch every minute, though; I've never forgotten the look on his face the day he shot the deer. It could just as easily have been me.

It's hard to know how paranoid to be. Both Rich and Barbour are consistent in subtly mentioning my "roots" at least one out of three times they say anything to me at all. The only person I know who relates to being nonwhite is Georgia, and she tells me that while she never forgets her heritage, her job on the planet is to be a voice for children, and that's what she concentrates on first. "But I'm over forty," she says, "and you're almost eighteen. It's one of those things you have to figure out for yourself. Things will look different when you get to college. The inland Northwest isn't exactly the most ethnically balanced spot in the universe." For the most part it's not something I spend a lot of time with except when I hear some off-the-wall remark from Barbour, or when Rich Marshall is messing with my head. I said earlier the Aryan Nations fort is about forty miles from Spokane, in the Idaho Panhandle at Hayden Lake. Neo-Nazis from all over the country come there to "summer camp," where they have war games and spout mindless slogans of racial purity. Sometimes they obtain a parade permit and march through the streets of Coeur d'Alene or congregate in Riverfront Park in Spokane. On the surface these guys look like a bunch of bozos. The Reverend Butler, the geezer who runs it, is articulate enough, but he's crazier than an outhouse rat. And the smartest of the guys who show up for that camp can draw maybe one out of three swastikas correctly. I drove to Spokane to observe one of their rallies last year for a journalism story, and more than anything they looked ridiculous. I said that in the article, but Dad read it and asked if I knew that the guy who opened fire in a Jewish day care in Los Angeles a few years back had ties to those guys. Or whether I was aware a Jewish radio-talk-show host in Denver was gunned down by people traced back to this group. Or that a guy coming from somewhere in the South to support Randy Weaver, the white supremist who held off the FBI at Ruby Ridge, shot two people in the Spokane bus station just because they were a mixed couple. He didn't want to alarm me, he said, but he wanted me armed with the facts.

Truth is, I wouldn't give any of that a second thought—except when I went to cover the story, I swear I saw Rich Marshall standing in the middle of the park talking with one of the "officers." They were whooping it up like old buddies. That didn't surprise me all that much, and to tell the truth I couldn't care less generally; he has the requisite I.Q.

But the next day he catches me just after I've said good-bye to Carly in Wolfy's parking lot and pulls his pickup in close just after I open my car door, trapping me. He says, "Hey, Jones."

"Hey, Rich."

"Hypothetical question."

I take a deep breath, appear disinterested. "What, Rich?"

"Let's say you got married and had a family. And let's say the Department of Children's Services made up a bunch of bullshit to keep you away from your wife and kids." He waits.

"Okay," I say, "let's say that."

"And let's say you find out some guy who ain't got *no* business within ten miles of your family gets himself involved."

"Okay."

"What do you do with him?"

"Nothing, Rich. I just do whatever I have to do to get back with my wife and kids."

"Not me," he says, pointing his trusty forefinger at me, bringing his thumb/hammer down. "Not me."

I shrug and get into my car, waiting for him to pull back so I can close the door, and then sit there waiting for the adrenaline flow to ebb.

Ten minutes later at All Night, I tear the water *up*; swim two-hundred-yard repeats leaving every three-and-a-half minutes until I can barely drag the paddles through the water, forcing my elbows high through each stroke, sending deep burning pain into my shoulders and chest, trying to replace the fear and contempt in my gut. Maybe this is Rich Marshall's purpose in my life, to make me faster.

An hour and a half later I drag my dripping butt out of the

water and head for home, only to rise—now more pissed than scared—around four to return for some distance work before the rest of the guys show for the station workout, and find Icko waiting for me.

Icko is Interim Coach Oliver's new acronym. Yesterday I started calling him our I.C.O., but when Chris Coughlin heard it he was convinced I was spelling the name so he wouldn't understand something, like they do at his home. I tried to explain about acronyms, but that went about as far over his head as you can go without escaping gravity, and he started calling Oliver Icko. As I tried to explain it for the tenth or eleventh time, Oliver overheard me and said, "Hey, I like it. *Icko.* It has a certain ring."

I said, "Yeah, like already chewed food, or snot running into your mustache. Ick-O!"

Icko told me to watch it.

At any rate, when I show up now, a little after four, he's already up. "You got a minute, chief?" He follows me to the pool.

I say, "What's up?"

"I been watching what you call a swim team pretty close," he says, "and no matter how hard I watch, it don't look like any swim team I ever saw."

I said it was a little raw.

"Raw? Hell, I seen open, seeping sores ain't as raw as this team. Ever notice you're the only actual swimmer? Hell, you look like one of them boys in the O-lympics."

I tell him it's the same principle as my parking my Chevy Corvair next to some *really* ugly cars in the school parking lot. He says I couldn't find an ugly enough car to make a Corvair look Olympic, but he gets the point.

"There some kind of vendetta goin' on at school about this team?"

80

"What do you mean?"

"Well," he says, "you know the Barbour kid, the one that works for Marshall Logging in the summer? The football stud?"

"Mike," I say. "Mike Barbour. Yeah, I know him."

"I seen him stacking up little slow Chris back behind the hardware store."

Shit. "Did he hurt him?"

"Naw," Icko says. "I done what I used to do with my boy."

"What was that?"

"Picked me up a piece of rebar."

"You used to hit your kid with rebar?"

Icko laughs. "Never thought of that. Naw, I just stood there talking to him real reasonable, you know, sayin' he ought to increase his circle of friends enough to include people like my friend Chris there, while I bent the rebar into a horseshoe. He seemed to understand."

"Was Chris okay?"

"Yeah, I guess. You know how he don't say much. Well, he was sayin' less than that. He liked the rebar thing, though. 'Cept he thought it was a magic trick. Asked me to teach it to him."

I ask Icko if he knew why Barbour was bugging Chris in the first place.

He says, "Somethin' about a letter jacket. I didn't understand. I mean, the kid was wearin' that Speedo jacket he always wears."

Man, Mike Barbour is a one-trick pony.

So later in the morning I'm "doing lunch" in Simet's room, bringing him current on the progress of his semi-landlocked mermen, advising against his applying for the job with the men's national team.

He says, "What are your goals?"

"A small cattle ranch outside Albuquerque," I tell him. "A few longhorns—"

"For the season," he says.

"Swim as fast as I can. Get the gold."

"That it?"

"Letter jackets for the downtrodden, one and all."

"That's still the big deal to you, isn't it?"

"Still is."

"Coach Benson caught me in the teachers' lounge this morning," he says.

"You must have been delighted."

"Not particularly. He was feeling me out for swim team letter requirements; said he thought it was great I was getting a team going, though I should have talked you into going out for football if I really wanted to do the school a favor, rather than create a whole new sport for you."

I love that they all want me. "What did you tell him?"

"I told him I didn't create swimming; it's been going on a long time. Told him about a couple of guys named Schollander and Spitz."

Simet's as big a smartass as I am.

"He said he knew the letter requirements were up to me, but he hoped I wouldn't diminish what it means to be a Wolverine. Mike Barbour's name came up, along with a couple of other ball players; and yours, of course. Said they were concerned that you were trying to make a sham of it."

"It's already a sham. I'm just exposing it."

"You got something going on with Mike Barbour?"

I shrug.

"Well, I don't know exactly what this is all about, but remember I have to live here after you're gone. We can be creative, but I have a certain respect for athletics myself, so don't push it *too* far."

I promise I won't push it too far. But like I said, Simet's one of those guys who remembers what it was like to be a kid, so I figure "too far" is quite a ways out there.

7

Finally Andy Mott shows. I believe I may have mentioned I wasn't exactly looking forward to that. You know how that Li'l Abner character goes around with a cloud over his head all the time? Well, Andy's cloud is three times the size and shudders with thunder and lightning. Andy seldom talks; the cloud speaks for him.

He limps onto the deck in that unique gait one morning, dressed in gray sweatpants, Nikes, and a T-shirt. His torso cuts an impressive figure; he ain't Tay-Roy, but he isn't Chris Coughlin, either. This guy has spent some time pushing iron away from gravity.

He whips off the T-shirt, kicks off his shoes as he sits on the bench, pulls off his sweatpants, then unstraps his right *leg*. The guy has a prosthesis from just above the knee. He shoves it behind the bench, hops over to the end of the pool, and stands.

Andy Mott is a junior, moved here two years ago, and *no*body knows he's missing a body part. He says, "What's the workout?"

I almost can't tell him we're doing kicks.

He looks at me with contempt, or maybe that's just his look, and says, "My best thing," and hits the water.

Everyone is stunned, but Chris is paralyzed; wide-eyed with mouth agape, staring first at Andy in the water, then at the leg, a space-age metallic thing, then back to Andy. Communication with Chris Coughlin teaches one patience. There is a standard two-second lag time between input and output. Even with the simplest of questions, you watch his eyes and see the wheels slowly turn. His brain has a standard transmission, as if he has to create his own synapses. That's for a simple question. When some guy limps into the pool and takes off his leg before diving in, Chris's wiring tangles irreparably.

I have to admit it frays the ends of my own, but I walk Chris over to the bench and start him swimming on the surgical tubing, though he almost breaks his neck craning it to see if Andy's for real.

At the end of workout, Andy pulls himself out of the water, hops over and straps on the leg. Chris still can't take his eyes off him. Andy looks up and says, "What's the matter, never seen a one-legged swimmer before?"

After the standard hesitation, Chris shakes his head slowly and says, "Huh-uh."

I couldn't be happier. Before Andy actually turned up, I believed the Magnificent Seven consisted of one swimmer of color, a representative from each extreme of the educational spectrum, a muscle man, a giant, a chameleon, and a psychopath; when in fact we have one swimmer of color, a representative from each extreme of the educational spectrum, a muscle man, a giant, a chameleon, and a *one-legged* psychopath. When I envision us walking seven abreast through the halls of Cutter High, decked out in the sacred blue and gold, my heart swells.

By the time Thanksgiving vacation is over and Simet is legally coaching, we are a well-oiled machine. We have three in the water and four on the benches at all times. I'm putting in extra yards during off hours and my repeat times are getting faster daily, and if *my* times are in rapid descent, the other guys' times are in freefall. Fifteen minutes of simple stroke technique per day will make a nonswimmer exponentially faster, and Simet is truly a master technician.

Dan Hole benefits most from that because he is first and foremost a student, and the very physics of swimming fascinates him. Jackie Craig, who remains the team's ghost, listens intently to Simet's every word, watches Dan put those words into practice, then imitates Dan's every move. Though he's been with us for weeks, I don't think Jackie has uttered three sentences. I look back and realize I haven't even thought of him and wonder if his whole life is like that. He shows up, watches, imitates, all the time remaining invisible. Mott comes in every day looking surly, leaves looking surly, and does everything in between with a barely controlled rage. I believe if the water were alive, he would beat it to death. Chris doesn't get much from the technique instruction, but once or twice a week Simet gets into the water with him and manually moves his arms and legs correctly through the strokes. Chris probably has the best natural stroke on the team, and that's a good thing, because no matter how much Coach works with him, that stroke doesn't change. Simon continues to churn the water in search of muscle definition.

Tay-Roy probably has the most overall talent next to me. Though not a natural, he has an okay feel for the water, and as he alters his body design from bodybuilder to swimmer, he gets better and better. He's the one guy who knows what it means to dedicate himself athletically. I don't know how many people understand the dedication bodybuilding takes, or what it takes to bring yourself to the musical level Tay-Roy has achieved. Even I can learn from him. He is singular in his vision of himself as an athlete.

The first day Simet is on the job, Icko tries to disappear, standing over by the door for most of the workout, then slipping out early. The second day, while I'm moving from the water to the benches, I grab his arm and bring him to Coach. "Oliver Van Zandt," I say, by way of introduction.

Simet sticks out his hand. "Pleased to meet you, Mr. Van Zandt. I didn't realize that was you. I understand I have you to thank for keeping this group together."

"They were pretty much together already, I was just around," Icko says. "And you can call me Icko."

Coach says, "Not the way I heard it, Icko."

"I don't know much about swimming," Icko says. "In fact, I don't know *nothin'* about swimming."

Coach glances around the pool. Jackie Craig and Chris Coughlin lie flat on their stomachs, stroking away on the benches to the beat of Bob Seger's "Betty Lou's Gettin' Out Tonight," while Tay-Roy churns the water in his lane like a washing-machine agitator, and Simon DeLong displaces enough water on his dive to wash Dan Hole to the far side of one lane and Mott to the side of the other. "You're not the only one here who doesn't know much about swimming, sir. And I'd sincerely appreciate it if you were to stick around as my assistant. I'm sure there's money in the budget to compensate you."

"Hell," Icko says, "I got two full-time jobs as it is. No reason to pay me for this. I kind of enjoy it."

"I kind of enjoy it, too," Simet says, "but they still pay me."

As I'm moving to the benches, I hear Simet ask him if he can drive a school bus. *That* would make us one self-contained traveling water show.

I look at us: a group of real outsiders, a group Cutter High school has offered very little to. You could make a case for the fact that Cutter has offered me a *lot* and that I've simply refused to take it, but for whatever reason, I fit better here than I've fit anywhere before. It's hard to put my finger on, maybe it boils down to the racial piece. It isn't as if I live in a city where racial struggles are everyday issues if you discount people like Rich and Mike Barbour, and it isn't as if I'm carrying much personal cultural history, though my parents have always kept me supplied with books about African-American heroes, and we've always celebrated certain of their accomplishments and birthdays. But the fact is, my parents are white and the only others close to my "persuasion" are a child therapist and a preschooler. Sweet Georgia Brown, more by example than by lecture, has continually demonstrated that racist thought and action say far more about the person they come from than about the person at whom they are directed. Yet, no matter what you *know*, it doesn't always alter how you *feel*.

When I was eight, in the third grade, I learned about Charlotte Volare's birthday party the day after, when one of my friends asked why I wasn't there. I walked up to Charlotte and asked her the same thing. She said her parents didn't want me in their house because I wasn't white; that her grandfather had been killed by some Japanese people in this thing called World War II, an event neither of us could quite pin down. It was okay for her to play with me at school, but she could never *ever* kiss me or have me to her house. I was pretty hurt, and Dad offered to call up Mr.

88

Volare to find out what gives, but Charlotte was gorgeous beyond belief, with large, round brown eyes, and dark, thick hair that spilled down to the middle of her back like a luxurious blanket. Even at eight, I was pretty sure if my biker dad jumped in the middle of Mr. Volare's shit I could kiss good-bye any idea of becoming Charlotte's secret boyfriend, so with Georgia's help I talked him out of it. But the sting was undeniable. Charlotte was so matter-of-fact with her explanation that I thought there really *was* something different and wrong about me that everyone else took for granted.

"Not a thing wrong with you, baby," Georgia said over a plate of those miraculous cookies when I showed up at her house, crying and majorly pissed. "Some people's parents are just stupid and mean; so mean they would cheat their own children out of having a great friend like you. Got to feel bad for that Charlotte." By the time that conversation was over, I half felt bad for Charlotte.

So as an outsider, I may rate only a three or four on a scale of ten, where Dan might be a six, Simon and Chris an eight, Jackie—who knows?, Tay-Roy wherever he puts himself (he goes his own way), and Mott a fifty. Andy is famous as the king of in-school suspension, out-of-school suspension, and Saturday school; he spends more time in those places than in the classroom. We know he accrues most of that time not from fighting, but from calling to public attention Morgan's shortcomings as a principal, or pointing out some teacher's personal deficits in front of the class. While he hasn't said a cross word to Simet or Icko, nor to any of us for that matter, he is notorious for the level of vitriol in his parting comments. I haven't yet figured out why he picked this team for his sanctuary.

* * *

89

Cutter High School has many rituals I could do without, but none is more annoying than the special assembly before each new athletic season. The athletes from the teams are introduced, and the captain and coach have to make a short speech about team goals and what it means to compete for Cutter.

We operate on a shortened class schedule that day, so the assembly lasts the entire final hour. Winter sports include basketball, wrestling, volleyball, gymnastics, and now swimming. To this, I have not been looking forward. We will parade our band of merry men before a crowd of over seven hundred students that includes the members of the state champion football team.

The other teams have a large number of returning lettermen, so the gym floor is covered with blue and gold by the time we are introduced, dead last, fitting for the spot we are sure to place in the conference. Icko has taken an hour off work and follows Simet onto the floor decked out in his Burger King uniform. I'm behind him, followed by Chris Coughlin, who is so seriously traumatized by having to walk in front of that many people that I have to keep saying, "Stay with me, Chris. Stay with me, Chris. Chris?" I hear the laughter and turn around to see Jackie Craig run into him because Chris has stopped when someone in the bleachers calls out, "Dummy!" A moment later we watch a teacher hauling the culprit out, but Chris is still paralyzed and Jackie's nose is bleeding from the collision. I take Chris's arm, bring him next to me, and tell him to stare just above the top bleacher and hum "Rudolf the Red-Nosed Reindeer" in his head.

Simet introduces us as a new team with a good chance of getting points at State to help Cutter out with the all-sport state championship. When he introduces Icko, several people shout out orders for a burger and fries. Then I'm introduced as captain to a mixture of cheers and boos. I'm fairly popular, but there's not a student in this school who doesn't know I'm considered a slacker for not turning out for football and basketball. My speech is short. I tell them our goal is to finish the season with as many swimmers as started. Mott picks up a couple of days of I.S.S. when he hears somebody snicker at his name and gives the entire crowd a double middle-digit salute.

All things considered, we weather it pretty well.

The experience starts me obsessing on the idea of embarrassment and humiliation. Truth is, I have no idea how I stack up against the rest of the swimmers in the state, don't even know who the best ones are. I downloaded last year's best times off the Internet, but I still can't get a fix on where my times fit; I get an extra turn each hundred yards because we're swimming in a twenty-yard pool, give or take a couple of feet for the underwater shelf that also prevents me from flipping turns at that end. For a sprinter, starts and turns are absolutely crucial. All I can do is work out as hard as I possibly can, and start checking my times against the best times after our first meet, which isn't until after Christmas vacation. Meantime, the trick is to get in as much distance as possible so I can avoid both embarrassment and humiliation.

That evening, just after I drop off Carly to head home, having completed a science experiment with steam and the interior of a Chevy Corvair, a car pulls up close on my tail. I'm just paranoid enough to know it's got to be Rich Marshall or one of the jocks from the football team, ready to let me know one thing or the other about letter jackets or patriotism to good old Cutter High. So I drive around awhile, through some tougher parts of town, back and forth down some alleys. Out by the old cemetery I try to ditch whoever it is, inching through the graveyard itself, then accelerating as quickly as a Corvair can without dropping the engine onto the street. My evasive action doesn't have the same effect of James Garner's Camaro in the old *Rockford Files* TV show, and I finally pull up in front of my house, jump out, and rush back before whoever it is can get their driver-side door open, then prop my knee against the door, ready to do whatever business is needed.

The window rolls down slowly, and I'm face-to-face with Judy Coughlin, Chris's aunt. She says, "Goodness, were you lost?"

I know nothing about this woman except that she took over for Chris's mother when Chris came out of the hospital after the Saran Wrap incident. Before that, when he lived with his mom, any bad guy who wanted to got his hands on that kid and did what they wanted. I look at him sometimes in the water, think of what a stud his half-brother was, see that natural stroke, the possibilities that might exist for him if he didn't have to wait almost a full second after I say go to actually jump in the water.

I start to make up some wild story to explain my circuitous route home, before realizing a couple of sentences into it that I must sound like the goofball of the universe. "Never mind," I say. "I'll pay you money not to tell my dad."

"I just wanted to thank you," she says.

"For what?"

"You know, for taking my nephew onto your swim team." She looks tired, and grateful.

I say, "Hey, I need him more than he needs me. He's not going to be a bad little swimmer."

"He's been in school twelve years," she says. "This is the first time in eleven years anyone has paid one bit of attention to him, other than to make him drink urine out of a Seven-Up can or trick him into giving a dog an erection."

I know all the Chris Coughlin stories. His hard times have come at the hands of teachers as well as kids, some of them not nearly as major as the Seven-Up incident, but just as devastating in the long run. Through the years Chris was always with our class part of the day, being mainstreamed in art and music, and of course he was present for class functions like Christmas parties or class plays.

In fifth grade our teacher was a guy named Sanford Davis. That year was the first most of us had a man teacher, and we were pretty excited about it, ready for someone to challenge our budding masculinity. But Mr. Davis wasn't exactly the hands-on mountaineer we had in mind. He was the new preacher at the Mountain Bible Center, and he ran his classroom the way I imagine he ran his church, with a holy iron fist. He tolerated exactly zero bullshit in his classroom. We sat in rows, the person with the best grades in the front seat to his far left, moving down the academic gradient to Chris Coughlin in the back seat of the right-hand row. Every three weeks he went through his grade book and reseated us. The one person who never moved was Chris; his position was nailed down by a good twenty points. Davis often used him as an example of an "unfortunate" and threatened on a regular basis to put a student in a desk *behind* Chris, which I suppose would have had to be considered educational wasteland. He talked about Chris as if he weren't there, though most of the time it was hard to tell if that bothered Chris or not. He would hear his name, look up, then go back to what he was doing. I now know he felt every sting. He's slow, but he gets the basic stuff just

93

fine. Seven years later the mention of Davis's name brings a crinkle to his nose.

We were waiting for the designated Santa, and Davis was killing time having us make all the words we could out of the word Christmas. The concept of moving letters around to do that was beyond Chris, but he saw two right off; his own name and what he believed was Jesus' last name, and he wrote them down in that order.

Davis was pacing up and down the aisles, hands folded behind his back, smelling of Old Spice and trying to catch us cheating. He turned around at Chris's desk, ready to retrace his steps, noticed Chris's unpardonable sin, bent down and told him to reverse the order of the names. Well, the problem was that slow as he was, Chris has always gotten excited anytime he did something on his own, and having to change the order would mean he didn't do it right in the first place, and he dug in his heels and refused to budge. By God, he had found those two words by himself and they were right and he wasn't going to erase or scratch them out.

Davis said, "You can't put your own name before the name of the Lord."

Chris said this wasn't the name of the Lord, it was Jesus' last name.

Davis said they were the same thing; that lord was a title, like king.

That was *way* past Chris's ability to understand.

Davis tried to explain that Chris simply shouldn't put his name ahead of Jesus; it wasn't right.

Then Chris said the smartest thing that was said all day. He said they told him at Sunday school that Jesus liked kids and He was nice. So He wouldn't mind.

Davis made the mistake of saying Chris went to the *wrong Sunday school*, and Chris just sat there stupefied. Then Davis did the thing somebody should have shot him for; he made Chris stand up beside his desk, and he said, "Chris Coughlin thinks he's better than Jesus."

Davis didn't know that Chris's brother took Chris to Sunday school each week, that now Davis was treading on holy ground. Chris spun out, screaming that Davis was a liar, that *nobody* was better than Jesus and he did not go to the wrong Sunday school and he would be glad to bring his brother in here to kick Davis's ass for saying that.

I got to escort him to the office, and he spent the next minutes trembling and trying to explain how he wasn't better than Jesus and he went to the right Sunday school because his brother took him and his brother would never take him to the wrong one. Of course nobody there knew what he was talking about, and in the end, Chris Coughlin missed the Christmas party. Another day in the life . . .

I look at his aunt now, standing next to her beat-up Dodge Dart. She looks small and helpless, kicked by the world. "Really," I tell her. "Chris could be a real swimmer if he stays with it."

She smiles. "He'll stay with it as long as there's somebody like you to watch over him. He says you're his hero. He'd do anything for you. It's a moment for him. He doesn't get very many moments. I just wanted to thank you."

Before I can say another word, she is back in the Dart, driving down the road.

Man, what kind of a fucked-up world is this? You should have to be a lot more than decent to be a kid's hero.

8

Practices go better than I could have imagined through Christmas vacation. We're still holding two a day, and all seven of us show for every one. Chris actually gets used to Andy sliding his leg under the bench before each workout, and at one point he sneaks over and touches it. Icko uses what little free time he has to study for his Class II driver's license so he can drive the bus, for which the school district will pay him. He turns into our utility guy, coaching out-of-water activities and doubling as team psychologist ("You want to turn out like everyone thinks you've already turned out?"), tripling as manager in charge of making sure Chris always knows where his swimming suit and goggles are and that he isn't terrorized by the existence of Andy Mott on the team or on the planet.

Our first road trip, which takes place on the second weekend back from vacation, sets the stage for our season. It's an evening double-dual meet between us and two Idaho schools, which means it doesn't count in the conference standings. Swim teams are spread pretty thin throughout eastern Washington and northern Idaho, so the travel can be grueling. We'll be on two-lane blacktop most of the way, and the sky begins spitting snow as we prepare to leave. Icko, who has come straight from his job at Burger King, disappears into the school and returns with two burlap bags filled with tire chains, throws them into the back of the bus, and calls all aboard. Neither of the district's two minibuses is available for the trip, so we're traveling in what seems like a 747.

Mott puts on his headphones as he steps onto the bus, walks back to the last seat and lies down, disappearing from view. The rest of us, plus Simet, fill in the first three rows behind Icko and bring out the cards and Game Boys and reading material. It's a seventy-mile trip that will take about two hours, given terrain and road conditions.

When we've been on the road fifteen or twenty minutes, I lean forward and tap Simet on the shoulder. "You ever figure out the letter requirements?"

He grimaces. "I was supposed to have them up for consideration by the Athletic Council before the first meet," he says. "I put them off until the first *conference* meet."

"I have an idea."

"Shoot."

"How about anybody who hits his best time each time he swims, gets a letter."

He frowns. "You kidding me?"

"No, man, listen. This is perfect. Remember what it was like when you started swimming? You got faster by the week, just from the competition and the increased workouts and stroke technique. Seriously, I hit my best times every week for a couple of years when I started. Almost everyone did."

He considers. "That was a long time ago," he says. "I can't be sure."

"They probably didn't have clocks back then, but trust me, it's true. And here's the beauty of it. The Athletic

Council will never figure it out. I mean, if you asked the track team to do that, no one would letter."

Simet smiles. "You might be right. I'll tell them I could choose an arbitrary number of points, but that might be too easy because a lot of teams will have only one entry per event, and my guys would pick up too many easy points." He thinks a minute longer. "One thing, though."

"What?"

"You don't tell any of these guys until after we swim tonight. I want them going all out for their first meet, so we know we're getting the most out of them the rest of the season."

"Fair enough."

About a half hour from our destination, Coach walks back and slips Mott's earphones off, calls for everyone's attention. "Listen up," he says. "How we do in this first meet sets the stage for the rest of the year, sets our goals. I want you to close your eyes and listen to me." He pauses. "That's everyone but you, Icko."

Icko laughs. "Got my eyes on the road, boss."

"Okay, the rest of you. Picture this. It's a big school, a couple of years old. Two stories. The pool is at the west end. We enter through the north side of the gym and walk across the basketball floor to the lockers." He goes on to describe the place in detail, from the lighting to the electronic timing pads, the coaches' office, even the lifeguard stands. He wants us to visualize it, he says, because he wants it to be familiar. Nothing new or big or scary. The pool is longer, so we'll have to get used to that during warm-ups, but remember it means fewer laps. There'll be good swimmers, but they'll have some guys who are new, also. Since we don't know how we stack up, we just go out and hit the best times we can. Nothing we do tonight will be wrong. We're just discovering who we are as swimmers.

"A double-dual meet is exactly what it sounds like. We swim against each team individually. It's as if we're swimming two meets. So we could lose to one team but score points against another. Again, just swim as hard as you can and have some fun. We'll hit the pizza place on the way out of town." Again he pauses. "Okay, anyone have any goals they want to state for everyone to hear?"

From the back of the bus, Mott says, "My goal is to not assault anyone with my leg for laughing at it."

"That would be good," Simet says. "Assaulting the entire student body with your middle fingers is about as far as I stretch. Besides, I don't carry bail money with me."

Icko yells back to him, "Besides, this is Idaho. Even swimmers are required to carry guns."

Chris's eyes widen. "There's guns?"

Simet laughs and ruffles his hair. "Icko was teasing. No guns on this one, Chris. Not even the starter has a gun here. They're newfangled."

Chris says, "Newfangled," and laughs. He's been obsessing about the starter gun since he heard such a thing exists. It does not help that Mott has been telling him if the starter is mad at his wife, sometimes he shoots a swimmer.

I have one goal, but it's for Tay-Roy: for him not to get sexually assaulted on the deck by the female spectators from either of the opposing schools. Man, that guy looks like a serious hunk in a tank suit. Tay-Roy says one of us is going to be disappointed because his goal is opposite that.

Dan Hole says he's going to use this meet to further study his personal kinesiology. Icko tells him to drop for ten.

Jackie Craig, who has disappeared while sitting right in front of us, says, "I just want people to still be in the water when I finish," to which Icko responds by shaking his head and whistling "The Impossible Dream."

Then we're all looking at Simon. He shrugs.

"Come on, Simon," Coach says.

Simon starts to talk, but his voice deserts him and a tear wells up in his eye. He shrugs again, and we look up to see Mott limping up the aisle. He sits beside Simon, albeit with his back to him, knees in the aisle. Mott looks at Coach. "How 'bout puttin' me an' DeLong in the same events?"

Coach thinks a second. "We could do that."

Mott grabs Simon's knee. "They'll think a one-legged asshole is a lot funnier than a fat guy." He gets up and limps back.

I watch him slip on the earphones as his head disappears below the back seat. He'd never want you to know it, but he's got some class.

The meet itself is an eye-opener. I'm in way better shape than I thought and take the hundred and two hundred freestyle pulling away. My times aren't world beaters, but they're very competitive for the beginning of the season, and I even blow one turn in the two hundred and still pull it out.

The kid in the lane next to me slaps the water after the hundred, and I'm sure I hear him say he's *never* been beat by a nigger, which for some reason doesn't ignite my will to hold his head under water till he passes out. I reach across the lane rope and grab his hand, like I'm shaking it, pull him close and whisper, "Get used to it."

Mott does his best to take the heat off Simon. After they call the hundred-yard breast stroke, just as Simon is about to shed his warm-ups, he tears off his sweatpants, jerks his leg off with a flair, and throws it over to me. If it were a gymnastic move, it would have received a ten, and the crowd falls dead silent.

There is a ten-minute delay at the end of the race because one of the judges can't determine whether or not Andy used a legal kick. In the breast stroke, a swimmer's legs have to kick symmetrically, and lo and behold, the rule book states *nothing* about one-legged swimmers. Dan Hole solves the problem by suggesting that since it's a double-dual meet, and since two swimmers on both teams beat them both, why don't they disqualify Mott against one team, giving third-place points to Simon, and not the other, giving third-place points to Andy. That is the way it finally goes down in the book.

Chris gets third-place points twice because he's swimming the five hundred free and the hundred individual medley against nobody else from our team, and Tay-Roy does the same in the hundred fly and the two hundred I. M. Jackie pulls down a pair of thirds in the fifty free and the hundred back. Those races are short enough that there are still swimmers in the water when he finishes, though he bumps his head hard enough on the third turn of his backstroke race not to notice.

The Idaho teams are from neighboring schools and have a rivalry going, as well as a lot of friendships because most of them swim on the same summer team. They're friendly but a little aloof, and I can't tell if that's because they aren't sure if we got off the bus on our way to Burger King, or if they think they might catch whatever we obviously have.

When it's over, we gather our things, shake hands with

the other swimmers (most of whom wish us good luck, knowing how badly we need it), and head for Pizza Hut, where Dan almost blows cerebral capillaries trying to convince Chris that ordering a twelve-inch will give him more pizza than two six-inchers. Bottom line is, Chris wants two pizzas, and that's what he gets. "He's more intelligent than we think," Dan whispers in defeat. "He almost understood that." Simon gets two pizzas, too, but he takes Dan's advice and makes them both twelve.

Andy declares this whole experience a real bonus for Chris, making the swim team and getting a math tutor in the mix. He says it like he says everything, with extra sarcasm, but Dan just says, "Darn tootin'."

We take our same bus seats, seats that will come to belong to us as the season progresses, and start the trip home through what quickly turns into heavy snowfall.

We're feeling good. We not only walked away from our first swimming meet with as many people as we went into it with, but we all walked away with points. Chris is so proud of himself we almost have to give him two seats, and Simon is so grateful at having stood on that starting block and not melted away with embarrassment that his relief is leaking all over the bus. Jackie Craig seems exactly as he did before we hit the water, but I tell myself even a ghost has to feel good about this. Icko tells Dan Hole he's so proud of him he'll give him a bonus of three big words on the way home, and Dan promptly uses up two: euphoric and rapturous, both to describe his current emotional state. Mott says little, but slaps Simon on the shoulder as he limps back for his seat, adjusting his headphones as his head again disappears from view.

In a short while the euphoria and rapture wear off and, except for the droning of the engine, the inside of the bus is like a dorm room. Simon sounds like he turned into a sputtering chain saw, and when they get in sync, he and Mott are dueling nostrils. Simet and I talk awhile, but before long he's drifted off, too, and only Icko and I see the storm turn to a blizzard as we slow to about twenty miles an hour. The flakes become so thick and heavy we seem to be disappearing through a white wall.

The small transistor radio hanging from the rearview mirror warns us to stay home by the warm fire for the evening. Winter storm warnings are posted through tomorrow.

I say, "Uh, Icko, did I hear him say the road we're on is closed?"

"Couldn't be," he says back. "We're on it."

"We okay?"

"Hell, yeah," he says. "Used to drive truck over the continental divide in a lot more weather than this. Rolled one of those babies all the way down a mountain once."

I tell him that doesn't exactly inspire confidence.

"Like to killed me," he says. "Law of averages says a guy doesn't have two of those in one lifetime."

As he says it, bright light fills the interior of the bus like the Fourth of July as the loud blast from the horn of a state snowplow brings everyone up in his seat, and Icko cramps the wheel hard to the right. He pulls it back quickly, but the bus begins to slide, and for a few crazy moments we whirl as if we're on the Scrambler carnival ride, then hear a *bang!* as the front fender smashes into the natural rock wall on our left, violently reversing our field back to the other side and over a six-foot steep embankment.

Simet is up and through the bus in an instant, checking

103

us for injuries. Mott limps up the aisle, slipping off his headphones. "Damn," he says. "I been on drug trips that weren't that good."

Chris's hands are frozen into grips on the back of the seat in front of him, eyes wide, paralyzed. Jackie sits in his seat, head immobile, glancing side to side, waiting for someone to tell him what happened. Tay-Roy slept through it and is just now looking around. Simon hyperventilates.

No one is scratched, but Icko informs us we are at the bottom of the ditch with the fender smashed against the right front tire and we're going *nowhere* on our own. "I got up to the road," he says, "an' it is nothin' but *white* out there. Gonna be here a while, men."

Chris glances around frantically, looking ready to go ballistic, but Simet is right there. "You've been camping before, haven't you, Chris?"

Chris says, "With Brian."

"Your brother."

"Yeah."

"Well, that's what this is. It's a camping trip."

Chris says, "I wish my brother was here."

"So do I," Coach says back. "But we'll have to do this camping trip without him."

"Gots to do everything without him," Chris says. "He's dead. They gots his picture in the trophy case, though. You seen it?"

"Every day," Coach says. "Your brother was in my class. Real smart guy."

Chris smiles.

Icko goes back out into the snow, returns in just a few minutes. "Plenty of fuel," he says, "and the engine's working, so we can keep warm. All the comforts of home, which is a damn good thing, 'cause we ain't going to the real one for a while. I put a flare up on the road, and we've got plenty more, but it's a good bet nobody'll be by for a while." He holds his wrist near the speedometer light. "Close to midnight. Nobody's gonna miss us till two or so. Should have help by early morning."

The bus is equipped with an emergency pack that includes blankets, and we all have warm coats. Icko figures if we hang some of the extra blankets ceiling to floor about a third of the way back, we can keep the front part of the bus in the low sixties all night, running the engine intermittently.

Mott glances longingly to the back. "Sounds like I got to give up my seat." He looks around at us. "What the hell, no reason I can't come up here and see if I can pick up some social skills."

"If you can pick up social skills from *us*," Tay-Roy says, "you are in serious deprivation."

"He double flagged the student body," Simet says. "He's plenty deprived."

A hint of a smile crosses Andy's face in the green glow of the dash lights. I've never seen him smile before.

We hang the blankets and settle in. Coach says he and Icko will take care of the flares and the heat, that we can relax and get some sleep. "We're the only ones getting paid," he says. "And when this makes the papers, we'll be taking the credit for saving your lives."

"It'll be on page twelve," Simon says, "when they find out who you saved."

We sit with our backs to the windows, legs on the seats, struggling to get comfortable, and little by little the bus settles into silence. Icko starts the engine a couple of times while Simet hustles up to replace the flares. In the silence Mott says, "What if this is it for you guys?"

I say, "What do you mean?"

"What if I'm the only one to make it out? What if snow fills up this ditch and covers the bus, and I'm the only one smart enough not to be buried alive? Who do you want me to kill when I get back?"

"Find the guy operating that snowplow," Icko says. "He didn't even look back to see what happened to us."

"He must have figured we squeezed by," Simet says. "Those guys are pretty good about helping folks out when there's trouble."

"Well, we're in trouble, and he ain't helpin'," Icko says. "If I got to freeze to death, and the boy's got a killin' heart, that guy's got my vote for now."

I check to see if this conversation is freaking Chris out, but he's fast asleep.

"How 'bout you, Coach?" Mott says. "What if you had a freebie?"

"Can I just have them maimed?" Coach asks. "Do I have to go for the whole package? I have this brother-in-law. . . ."

"Nope," Mott says. "Got to be terminated."

"Have to take a rain check then," Simet says. "Somebody's got to support my sister."

Mott says, "DeLong?"

Without hesitation, Simon says, "My mom."

A brief moment of *dead* silence. "Care to elaborate on that?"

"Nope."

Jesus.

"How 'bout you, O silent one?" he says to Jackie.

Jackie shrugs.

"Didn't anyone ever tell you to use your *mouth* to talk?" Mott says. "Your shoulders are for your arms to hang off. You got to speak up, Jackie boy. Otherwise how do I know who to waste?"

Jackie shrugs again.

"We'll come back to you," Mott says. "Be thinking. Muscle man, what about you?"

"Nobody pops to mind," Tay-Roy says. "Maybe I'll give you my proxy. I have a feeling you have a long list."

"That I do, Popeye. That I do. Jones?"

"I'm into *saving* lives," I tell him. "So I'll have you waste yourself. First. That way I save all these others."

"Half-black guy around these parts?" Mott says. "Shit, you should have a list that stretches to Seattle. Think you'd rather be a one-legged white boy, or a black guy with everything in working order?" He nods toward Simon. "Or a fat guy." Toward Chris, "Or a dummy." And Jackie, "And . . . whatever that is."

Simet says, "That's enough."

"Isn't that why you want us around?" Mott says, ignoring him. "Give you a little edge on superiority?"

I say, "Mott, I didn't ask you to swim."

"Naw, you didn't. I'm here of my own volition." He looks at Dan. "Volition, you like that word, Hole?" He turns back to me. "I'm just checkin' out the nature of things. You know, how things are."

"Yeah, well, while you're checking them out, be careful what words you use." The heat is rising in me, adrenaline spilling over.

"So now you're the savior, too. Make sure nobody says anything bad about your team."

All of a sudden I have him by the collar, pulling him toward close. "No, *you* don't say anything bad about *our* team."

Simet's hand clamps on my wrist. "Let go, T. J."

Mott's and my eyes remain locked on each other. His stare is cold.

Simet says, "T. J." again, and I release my hold.

Simet says, "You check on 'the nature of things' on your own time, okay, Andy?"

Mott says, "Whatever."

Mott puts the headphones back on his head, settles into his seat. I stare out the window into the falling snow, wondering how I let him get to me. Maybe it's because he's partly right. I *did* go looking for guys who were out there a ways. Up until now, I thought it was pretty clever. Maybe I'm being an arrogant asshole. I consider that as the bus settles again into silence.

"Hey, man, don't worry about it." Mott's voice startles me. "Sometimes I just have to be a prick. Counselor says I have a personality disorder."

"It's okay," I say. "I mean, I don't know. Maybe you were right."

"Naw," he says. "I'm just good at making people think that."

"I don't know. The letter jacket thing—I've let myself get a little obsessed. I picked that, you guys didn't."

He dismisses that, is quiet a few seconds. Then, "Third guy after my dad left. On the off chance you make it out and I don't, he's the one I want offed. Canada Smith is his name. I got a trust fund for this leg. Get Canada Smith, and it's yours." He's quiet another few seconds. "Got to do it slow, though." Another moment of quiet. "Ol' Canada couldn't figure out which bed he was supposed to sleep in."

I'm speechless.

"I'd tell you the rest of that story, but we don't know each other that well." He laughs. "Maybe after the Olympic trials."

Snowflakes build on the windows. Other than Coach

slipping out to put out a new flare, or Icko intermittently starting the engine, there is nothing more than the sound of heavy breathing.

"You might decide you'd rather be a one-legged white boy than all brown an' shit," Mott says, after I've been sure he's asleep, "but believe me, you'd *damn* well rather be brown than be somebody got done by his mother's boyfriend."

I can't even imagine it, can't believe he's telling me.

As I think it, he says, "My counselor says the only chance I have is to tell people I'm a prick; that way I might have less reason to act like one." He settles down in the seat. "So, consider yourself told."

Around four the interior fills again with light, and an engine idles in the near distance. Icko is out the door, scrambling up the hill before most of us can clear our eyes, and before we know it, a state snowplow driver has us standing in the snow while he hooks a chain to the front bumper and hauls the bus to the highway. He and Icko pound the fender away from the wheel far enough to make it drivable, and we are headed through the snowy night, our first meet—and our first group therapy session—behind us.

9

We're famous in Cutter for a couple of days after "plunging off the treacherous, icy two-lane" and "surviving the wintry night," as the *Cutter Free Press* put it. Our team picture made the front page, and with the story slanted toward the events after the meet, the events *of* the meet were cleverly obscured.

The school paper took a different slant:

Cutter Mermen Set Records

In a performance this past weekend that may well rival the winning of the state football championship, the Cutter High School swim team set school records in nine individual events and one relay. Swimmers Dan Hole, Andy Mott, Jackie Craig, Simon DeLong, Tay-Roy Kibble, Chris Coughlin, and The Tao Jones scored points in those nine events in a losing effort. The small size of Cutter's team made winning either of the meets in this double-dual event virtually impossible. Cutter's team includes no divers, and their small numbers exclude them from participating in more than one of the two relays.

Nevertheless, the Herculean efforts of the small but fiercely competitive group of athletes could be the seed that spawns an athletic dynasty in the distant future, the likes of which Cutter High School has never known, according to team Captain T. J. Jones.

Coach John Simet was not available for comment.

A controversy arises over some of the syntax and word choices, but the reporter and the editor were able to convince the journalism teacher that certain journalistic license was in order to present the team in its most positive light. It may have helped that the editor and the reporter are one and the same, and the journalism teacher didn't actually see the article until the paper was published and in the hands of the student body.

Simet sits on top of his desk in the empty classroom a few minutes after the bell, reading and laughing while I stand by the door waiting.

He places the paper on his desk. "Man, I am going to, if you'll pardon the expression, eat shit over this."

I stare at my article. "You think?" I read a few sentences aloud. "Nothing there that isn't fact. I guess I could have played up Mott's disqualification, but why bust a guy when he's riding high?"

"Do you have any idea how Benson and Roundtree will respond to this? I've got to present our letter requirements at the Athletic Council meeting this afternoon. You'll be lucky if they don't require you guys to win every meet just to win a *lowercase* letter."

"Tell them I got out of control."

"They won't have trouble believing that."

"And that you're pissed; that you're requiring me to write a column next week about how facts can be used to present a different picture than what is true."

111

"It's just not in your nature to try to make my life easy, is it, Jones?"

I agree it is probably not in my nature.

I'm not in the hallway five seconds before I hear the melodic tones of Mike Barbour floating to my ears.

"Jones!"

I turn. He's with Rich Marshall, carrying the newspaper. "Saw this article on your swim team."

I say I'm glad he was able to get someone to read it to him.

"I got through it okay. Took me awhile, though. Kept stumbling over the word dynasty."

"It *does* have three syllables."

"That wasn't my problem," he says back. "My problem was with the *meaning*. I thought it meant something about winners. What was that, some Special Olympics swim meet?"

"You're welcome to get some of your football boys together for a little intramural meet," I tell him. "Say maybe as a fundraiser to get some of you guys tutors."

"We'll do a swim meet," he says, "if you guys wanna follow it up with a little flag football game."

Marshall clears his throat. Man, I feel like I've been transported to jock-monster hell. These guys are the worst of the worst. This isn't about athletics, this is about assholes. "Do you have any respect for anything, Jones?"

"Yeah, I have respect for some things," I say back, and have to hold myself back from saying I have respect for little kids and women and their right not to be treated totally like shit by some unconscious subhuman ass wipe.

"Like what?" he says.

"Nothing you'd recognize, Rich. Really, save your brain

112

cell for helping the PE teachers pick up balls after class. Maybe they'll let you keep a few of them so you'll have enough to figure out that a real hunter only murders adult animals." Man, I've got it going for these guys, more than I realized. I feel snakebit every time I'm around either of them.

"You better be a little careful what you say to me, Jones," Marshall says. "I'm the same as a teacher when I'm in the building. Don't make me report you."

"Report me, Marshall. Report me. Go tell Morgan I'm showing you nothing but contempt. Be accurate for once in your life. Do it next period. I've got a history quiz."

Barbour steps forward and my heart races. I can't *say* how much I want to mix it up; how badly I want to feel my knuckles buried in the cartilage of his nose, see blood splattered on the lockers. I don't even care whether it's his or mine. "You'll never see one of those goofballs you call swimmers in a Cutter letter jacket," he says. "Not one. You know who the male student rep to the Athletic Council is? You're looking at him, my friend of color. Off color." He grins.

"You guys just keep doing what you do," I say, my voice pinched as I walk away, slowly as if I couldn't give a shit; in fact I can barely breathe. I get upstairs and into an empty science lab, where I lean against the wall and talk myself out of going to the council meeting myself to tell them how screwed up it is to give a nothing-burger like Mike Barbour a vote on the athletic welfare of Chris Coughlin or Simon DeLong.

I don't have to run into Marshall more than once in a day to give myself permission to get out of the building for lunch. I invite Carly to my house for something to eat and anything else that might happen, since Mom is at work and Dad usually spends Wednesdays out at Head Start, but she has a paper due, so I drive over alone. This thing is getting out of hand, starting to mean too much. What will I do if Mike Barbour ends up with the deciding vote on our letter jackets?

Dad's car is in the driveway, so I figure I'll run it all by him; he's always good for an intelligent perspective. But I don't see or hear him inside. I pour a big glass of Gatorade and dig some cold chicken and potato salad out of the fridge, take it into the living room, and flip on Sports Center. Dad's coat lies across the back of the couch and his boots are under the coffee table; very unusual because my dad is a world-class neat freak. I mean, he can have a bike torn down in the garage and every tool is in its place before he stops to take a *leak*. Mom kids him about it all the time.

I holler "Dad" a couple of times, but except for the TV, the house is quiet. The guys on Sports Center seem determined to make me care about hockey, so I flip them off and wolf down my food, thinking I'll run up to my room for a short nap before I head back. I see the door closed to my parents' room, which is as unusual when they're not in it as the coat on the back of the couch, so I knock once and push it open.

The room is dark but for the flickering of the TV, where a group of humpback whales swim across the screen, emitting faint whale songs. A dark form fills the overstuffed chair in the corner by the dresser.

"Dad?"

No answer. I flip on the light. He sits, staring at the screen.

"Hey, man," I say. "What's going on?"

"Hey, T. J."

114

"You sick or something?"

"Something," he says. His beard is wet, eyes rimmed in red. "Turn the light off, will you?"

"Yeah, sure." I do. "Dad, what's going on?"

"Nothing. I'm fine. Just leave me alone, okay?"

I've never seen my dad like this. "Not okay. Come on, what's going on?"

He sighs. "Thirty years ago it happened," he says. "And sometimes it hits me like it was yesterday. Why didn't I look under the truck? It would have taken *three seconds.* Hell, if I'd checked for a flat I would have seen him."

I start toward him.

He says, "Don't. I'll be fine. You go on back to school."

"Dad . . ."

"I'll be fine. This happens every once in a while . . . you just haven't seen it. It'll pass."

"You sure?"

He says, "Go."

I'm not worth much in my afternoon classes; it's hard to see someone as big and strong as my father reduced like that. It makes me feel helpless to know that still happens. The guy is always there for anyone who needs him. He deserves better.

I'm in the locker room after school, getting into my sweats to take the bus ride over to All Night, my mind back in Dad's bedroom.

"Jonesey, Jonesey, Jonesey," Barbour says. "Looks like your coach jumped ship on you."

I snap into the present. "Oh, yeah?"

"We had the Athletic Council meeting."

"That right?"

"That's right. Wait till your Special Olympics squadron gets a load of your letter requirements."

"Save me the suspense."

Mott and Tay-Roy are headed for the door; they stop to listen.

"Simet went along with us; said it would be too easy for your boys to pick up points when there were no swimmers from the other team in some races. Got us to award the letter on 'personal improvement.' "

"Hey, we're improving. Why should that bother me?"

Barbour started to laugh. "Because it means you have to hit your best time every time you swim."

"What? That's not possible."

"Probably it isn't. None of you guys can swim *one race* slower than you did the time before. One bad race, no letter."

I say, "You're full of shit, Barbour. Simet would never do that."

"You can get the details from him." He points to Simet walking through the locker-room door.

I holler, "Coach!"

Barbour cackles. Coach looks up.

"Gotta ask you something." I hustle over and whisper, "Way to go."

The following meets are carbon copies of the first, except Icko keeps the bus on the road. I swim the fifty and hundred, or the hundred and two hundred, and win every time. The other guys swim whichever events will bring us the most points, establishing times in races they haven't swum before and bettering their times in those they have. As long as no one falls asleep in the water, we're all a good bet to

116

get faster and faster. Improved stroke technique alone will keep everyone in the running, not to mention the monster conditioning.

What I like about the meets more than the swimming, though, is the bus ride. When Icko pulls the door shut and fires up the engine, it feels almost cocoonlike. We talk about things we'd probably never mention in any other arena: Simon's mother drinks like a fish, Mott spent most of middle school in drug rehab, Tay-Roy lost a baby brother to SIDS, Dan Hole's father has heart trouble, Chris's aunt plays bingo, and Jackie Craig may or may not have a voice box. Simet and Icko let us talk, feeding questions once in a while to keep the conversation going, but never intruding.

It gets to be ritual; a half hour before we reach our destination, Simet begins going over each of our races, so between then and the end of the meet, we talk or think nothing but swimming. Then we stop at some local pizza place and, depending on how much time we have, eat there or take it on the bus with us.

Toward the end of the semester it becomes clear we may have problems with academic eligibility. "I've been doing the responsible thing," Coach says, walking to the back of the bus to remove Mott's headphones, "and it appears a couple of you are in danger of failing one or more classes. Mr. Mott is in danger of *passing* one. Hey, guys, this is serious business. You have to carry a two-oh average, and you have to be passing every class."

Mott says, "I'm going light on the academic thing this year."

Coach says, "You were until a minute ago. Now you're going heavy." He removes a folded sheet of paper from his pocket, holds it to one side to catch the light from the dashboard, squinting to read. "Mr. Hole, Mr. Jones, and Mr. Coughlin, you're all in great shape. Mr. DeLong, you are walking the edge in biology. Mr. Craig, you're three percentage points under in speech. Mr. Kibble, you don't seem able to remember your valences and the periodic table of elements in chem, and Mr. Mott, you are exactly one percentage point below passing in six classes." He stares at the page. "Mott, how do you do that?"

"It isn't easy, sir. I have to keep close track. Last week I got luckier than usual on an American history pop quiz and my grade slipped up over passing. Scared me."

"Well, if that scared you, prepare to be terrified, because before this semester ends, you are going to bring every one of those grades at least to a C." He turns to Jackie. "Mr. Craig, what is your problem in speech?"

Jackie shrugs.

"That might be it right there," Simet says. "Mr. DeLong?"

Simon says, "Biology is right before first lunch. I start seeing the things we're cutting up on my plate, and pretty soon I just have to get out of there."

Coach walks to the middle of the bus and retrieves a huge duffel bag from the overhead rack, dumps it onto the seat. "Icko, can you give me light back here for a sec?"

The dome light goes on. Simet rustles through the educational debris on the seat. "I took the liberty of getting the specifics from your teachers." He hands Jackie a copy of the periodic table, moving him to the seat across the aisle from Tay-Roy. "Enunciate each element loud and clear, Mr. Craig, as if you were delivering the Gettysburg Address. Mr. Kibble, when you hear the element, you will give Mr.

Craig back the symbol and valences. When you have them down one hundred percent, you may stop."

He hands Chris Coughlin a coloring book and a large box of crayons. "You said you like to color, right, Mr. Coughlin?" Chris's face lights up; he obviously *loves* to color. "Mr. Coughlin, since you are passing all your classes, I'm going to have you tutor Mr. DeLong. Do you know what a tutor is?"

Chris says, "Does he color?"

Simet nods. "He colors. In this case he colors guts." He hands Chris a biology coloring book; now where the hell do you suppose he got a biology coloring book? "Mr. DeLong will tell you which gut it is and what color to color it. If he tells you to color anything green, you yell to me."

Simet sits beside Dan Hole. "Mr. Hole, you have the toughest job. You are going to make certain that, for the first time in his life, Andy Mott passes all his classes with a C." He hands Dan a sheet of paper. "This is a list of Mott's missing assignments. We will take a chunk of time on each road trip, and tack on forty-five minutes to our workout time each day until the end of the semester. I'd like you to go over his assignments before he hands them in. Mr. Jones, you will play backup to Mr. Hole. If Mr. Mott gives him any trouble, hide Mr. Mott's leg."

For the rest of the trip, the periodic table of elements and their valences bounce off the walls in Jackie and Tay-Roy's voices, while Mott pumps Dan for answers and Dan tries for all he's worth to make Mott figure them out for himself. Chris takes instructions from Simon, meticulously coloring pictures of opened-up frogs and worms and cats and cows.

For the remainder of the semester the first forty-five minutes of workout takes place in Simet's classroom, and we get out of the water forty-five minutes later. When grades come out, though Mott has threatened Dan's life daily, we have the second-highest cumulative grade-point average of any winter athletic team and are all eligible.

The first day after semester break I read that my times in the sprints are among the top five in the state, and Simet is beginning to think not only can I get us points at the state meet, I could actually win something. We don't say that to anyone but each other.

"You're going to have a houseguest," Georgia says. I've been stopping over a couple times a week after practice to work with kids. I like that I always walk away from those sessions knowing something about myself I didn't know before. Georgia says I'm a natural, which is probably true because almost every kid she works with is referred from Child Protective Services and so has a history of loss. "Connection," she tells me over and over. "There is very little about humans that doesn't have to do with connection."

"What houseguest?"

"Heidi."

"No kidding?"

Georgia nods. "Her momma screwed up. Turned all her kiddies over to Rich for an entire afternoon. The caseworker placed them all immediately. The family they found for the boys couldn't take Heidi. She talks about you all the time. I called your daddy. You'll be good for her."

After all Rich has done, Alicia turns around and gives him the kids. Shit, Heidi isn't even *his*. "Think she'll be at our place a long time?"

Georgia shrugs. "That's the caseworker's call. Heidi was pretty freaked out after six hours with Rich and no one around to protect her. God knows what he said to her."

"When will she get there?"

"I'll take her in a little while," Georgia says. "Don't want to put any extra pressure on you, but she might be feelin' needy."

"Yeah, I'll keep an eye on her." I'm thinking this might be good for Dad. He always comes alive when there's a chance to help a kid. After seeing him in the bedroom, I'm beginning to understand why.

I stop at Wolfy's for a quick early evening Coke with Carly, so Heidi is home when I get there, sitting on the couch next to Georgia, facing the door, waiting. My parents have gone to bring back Happy Meals to celebrate.

Heidi is off the couch before I can get out of my coat, bounding across the room, leaping into my arms as if I'm her long-lost best friend. The impact almost knocks me over, and I'm choking in the tight grasp of her arms around my neck.

"Hey, Heidi," I say through a semiclosed windpipe. "What's up?"

"I live here," she says.

"Oh, yeah? Great. I need a sister. My parents like girls better than boys. I can get you to ask them for things I want."

Most of that goes over her head, and she glances back at Georgia.

"She was worried you wouldn't come," Georgia says. "She needs someone familiar. It's going to take time for her to get used to your dad, who basically looks like a serial killer."

I look at Heidi. "We'll have him eating out of our hands before sunup. He's the nicest mean-looking dad in the whole world."

Heidi's expression goes cold, and it takes me a second to

remember, with Georgia's help, that "dad" doesn't exactly conjure up the best images when your "dad" is Rich Marshall.

Mom and Dad return from Mickey D's with the Happy Meals, and Heidi wraps an arm around Georgia's leg to watch Dad bring them out of the sack. When he holds hers out to her, Heidi watches warily, but the image of Ronald McDonald and the smell of the greasy fries win out, and she steps up and takes it. She says, "Thank you," and seems to forget her fear once she gazes at the goodies inside.

Most kids have that same initial response when they first lay eyes on Dad, but he's great. He opens his Happy Meal slowly, peers inside with the same delight he sees on Heidi's face. She is meticulously careful, extracting one fry at a time, relishing each bite. Dad mimics her, but not in a disrespectful way, and soon she is smiling at him, sneaking peeks out of the corner of her eye.

And then it happens. As Heidi removes the bag of fries from the Happy Meal box, the sack catches on the edge of the lid and fries tumble onto the floor. She is instantly wide-eyed and horrified, glancing from the fries to my dad to the fries to Georgia. Tears squirt out of her eyes as she gasps, "I'll clean it up! I'm sorry! I'll clean it up! It will be okay!" and she is on her knees picking up the fries and putting them into the bag one by one, looking fearfully at my father.

Instantly he turns his fries onto the floor and drops to his knees with her. "We eat 'em down here all the time. That's how they're best." The panic drains out of Heidi as fast as it washed over her. She watches him with true joy. "Mmmmmmm," Dad says, picking up fries as fast as he can and stuffing them into his mouth. "I haven't had my fries like this for*ever*! I'm glad you reminded me."

Heidi starts to laugh, picks up a fry, and puts it carefully in her mouth.

What the hell, I dump mine, too, and suddenly the three of us are grazing over the living-room rug.

Mom shrugs her shoulders at Georgia, who says, "I think I brought her to the right place."

I walk Georgia to her car, where she turns and holds me by the shoulders. "Baby," she says, "it's a tall order for you to have this kid around; she adores you. I wouldn't do it, but she's fragile and you're the only other person to have made good contact with her besides me, though I think your dad may have made a big inroad just now."

I say, "What inroad? He always eats off the floor."

"She could stay at my place, but she has a real hard time letting me be with other kids; and if I can't be with other kids, I can't work."

"Don't worry about it. Dad and I'll have plenty of time for her. Maybe I'll get a Rich Marshall dartboard," I tell her, "and we'll have some fun."

I don't need a Rich Marshall dartboard because before I know it, I get the real thing. I guess he didn't get the message that Child Protection Services got a temporary restraining order to keep him away from Heidi, because he bangs on the door after midnight, loaded to the gills and groveling like the bottom feeder he is. I have the room next to the stairs on the second floor, so, by default, I greet all strangers in the night. Rich is the first, and I meet him on the porch. Apparently Alicia dropped out of his sight when she lost the kids, because Rich thinks she's here.

Man, these guys never fail to amaze me. They'll call any

name, exact any pain. They'll humiliate and slap and threaten to kill. Then the minute she leaves, he loved her more than life itself, is repentant for every bruise and scar, inside and out. He'll do *anything;* the remorse is without condition. Until the second she says no. Then he comes after her like a gut-shot badger.

That kind of behavior is pretty hard to understand, though it's been explained to me many times by my mother in regard to some domestic violence/abuse case she's tried in court. Though she understands it, she doesn't have a lot of time for it in anyone over three years old.

At any rate Rich Marshall is way past three years old. "I wanna see Aleeesha," he slobbers at me.

I say, "Alicia's not here, Rich."

"I know she's here. I gotta fin' her; tell her I'm sorry. I fucked up. I love her, man. Where's she at?"

"Go home, man."

"No, man, she's here. I know it. She's here with my kid. I need to tell her I love her."

"Heidi isn't your kid, Rich. And Alicia's not here. Maybe she's with the twins. Find out in the morning and you can call." I should know better than to argue with a drunk.

"I can't call her in the morning; they got a fuckin' no-contact order on me. I got to see her tonight."

"If they have a no-contact order," I say, "it's for day *and* night."

My efforts to keep this under control go up in smoke with the hardening behind his eyes. "You fuckin' my wife?"

"Nope. I have a girlfriend."

"Shit. You have a girlfriend."

"Strange as it seems. I'm not sleeping with your wife, Rich."

"She used to like your kind. Niggers or chinks or whatever."

"That would make me a chigger."

"Had little Heidi 'cause of one of you," he says. He's so drunk he doesn't remember I already know this. He glazes over a bit, sneering, maybe picturing Heidi's dad. "But she loves me now." As an afterthought, "Chigger. Tha's funny."

I say, "Sounds like you won Alicia for sure. Aren't you worried the cops will catch you here?"

"It's fuckin'—" and he holds his watch to the porch light, squinting— "after midnight. How would the fuckin' cops know I'm here?"

"Maybe because I called them when I heard you ring the doorbell." It's a lie, of course.

"You black asshole!" he yells. "You fuckin' black bastard asshole! You *are* fuckin' Aleeesha!"

He pulls up his T-shirt, exposing the butt of a pistol, but before he can even think of reaching for it, it is in my hand.

Rich stares at his belt, confused, as if the gun vanished into the hands of Merlin. He is *embalmed.* A whimper sounds behind me, and I glance around to see Heidi on the stairs, her raggedy, one-eyed stuffed otter in her hand.

"Nigger girl," Rich says. "Come here to me. Where's your momma?"

I move back, and she scurries to wrap her arm around my leg, staring silently at Rich as I holler for Dad, and light splashes across the floor as my parents' bedroom door opens and he barrels toward us. I don't care who you are; you could be Rich Marshall or Mike Tyson, but the sight of my old man coming at you out of the dark, bare chested with a baseball bat in his hand, is a daunting sight.

125

"This ain't over," Rich says. "Nobody fucks with my family."

"Looks like it's over for now," I say, but he is already headed down the walk.

I give Dad the pistol, and Mom and I sit with Heidi while he calls the police. I expect her to be scared, but all she can say is she wishes my daddy had given old Rich a good whack with that bat. We decide we will call my father the Louisville Slugger from now on. Heidi thinks that's pretty funny.

When we have her back in bed, I tell my parents Rich thinks I'm having sex with Alicia. "I barely even know her," I tell them.

"That doesn't matter," Mom says. "Don't fool with him. The last thing in the world you want is to be in Rich Marshall's cast of characters. He's a stalker, pure and simple, and stalkers believe what they want to believe. You don't even want him *thinking* your name."

"Too late for that. He uses it in vain every day at school."

"Well, I'll be on the phone at seven-thirty in the morning," she says. "And if Rich Marshall spends one more hour in that school, they'd better have a hell of an attorney."

"Cops will pick him up tonight," Dad says. "We won't have to worry about that for a while."

I tell them I'm not afraid of him even a little bit. In fact I'd welcome the chance.

Mom puts her hand on my knee and grips it hard enough that I feel heat. "Listen to me, T. J. You might be stronger and quicker now, but men like Rich are relentless, and they'll come after you in ways you can't imagine. If he believes you're taking something that belongs to him, he's as dangerous as they come. I see men like him in court every day."

I say I'm pretty familiar with the way Rich Marshall operates.

"You think you are, but this is completely different from him shooting that deer. That was just mean. When he's in this spot, he's desperate, which means he imagines things, like you sleeping with Alicia. When he talks like that, he isn't telling you what he thinks, he's telling you what he fears. One thing you want to know about Rich Marshall is this: In his mind, what he fears is his worst enemy. Anything that makes Rich Marshall feel weak will bring him at you like a devil. At that point, it isn't about whether you can whip him, it's about whether you see him coming." She squeezes my knee again. "You listen to me, young man. If you're wanting to try out your testosterone, try it out on someone else."

Mom won't let me go to bed until I promise to keep my testosterone under control.

10

I catch my dad working in the garage on one of the old bikes, an older BMW with a sidecar. That one belongs to him; I remember riding all over the country beside him when I was a little kid. We still go out on it sometimes, only now I drive as often as not. He always looks great in his old World War I army helmet, long brown hair flowing back, mirrored sunglasses and full beard hiding his face, riding beside me like I'm his chauffeur.

We talk while he works and I hand him tools, my one mechanical competence.

He says, "Guess I freaked you out a little in the bedroom that day."

"A little."

He breathes deep, sets down his wrench, and turns toward me. "I'm not proud of that, T. J."

"I didn't know it was still that bad."

"Most of the time it's not. Just once in a while, when I'm not paying attention. Usually when I start feeling too good."

The next question, I'm almost afraid to ask. But we're here, and we're talking. . . . "What do you tell yourself about that day?"

He laughs; a laugh that says you've just asked him something he's asked himself a million times. "Different things," he says. "In the old days I told myself I was a worthless scumbag; that *no* trucker fails to look under his truck before he takes off. I told myself there was no difference between negligence and an intentional act; the result's the same."

"That's pretty rough."

"Yeah. Another few months of that, and I'd have taken a fast motorcycle into a big tree."

I wait for the rest.

"Now," he says finally, "I'm a little kinder to myself most of the time. I tell myself I learned an important lesson the hard way: that the universe doesn't make allowances for mental lapses or ignorance, but that maybe I'm a better man because I know that."

I tell him he is a good man, but he isn't looking for compliments and doesn't respond.

"Before that day, if I'd read a newspaper article about a guy who ran over a baby out of negligence, I'd have cursed him for his stupidity and figured he deserved whatever came of it. I'm a lot more tolerant of things I used to despise, a lot slower to draw the line between good and bad. I look at a guy like Rich Marshall, for example. Thirty years ago I'd have hated his guts."

"I'm thirty years behind you on that one."

Dad laughs. "Well, I'm still not going to let him get his hands on a kid if I can help it, but you don't get like Rich is by being treated well all your life. I knew his old man, and he was one rough son of a bitch."

"It's hard for me to think of it like that," I say. "I think of him shooting that deer or what it must be like to live with him. Nothing in me can like him. And guys like Barbour are just Marshall Lite. It's hard to see them as victims."

"No real reason you should," he says. "You have to see everyone in relationship to you. Just because you understand the shit in someone else's life doesn't mean you don't stand up for your own."

He works meticulously on the bike as he talks, touching the parts, turning them over in his massive hands with the same care he uses in choosing his words. "I guess you could say, in the long run that incident changed about everything I believed. So much of what I've done has been in response to it. When I get a chance to play with a kid like Heidi, like with the french fries, it's as if the universe is throwing me a bone, letting me earn my way back a little closer to balance. Giving her a place to live is a true blessing, way more for me than her."

He falls quiet, and I stay awhile, handing him tools and watching the care he puts into his work.

"Anyway," he says later, "don't get freaked out if you see me like you did in the bedroom. I'm just finding my way."

I picture him back in the room, staring at— "The whale tape," I say. "Why was that playing?"

He laughs again. "Ten or fifteen years ago I read an article in *Sports Illustrated* about this elderly couple who had spent their lives studying whales up close. They were two of very few people actually allowed out into the migratory paths of whales, and they spent time in the water with them. I don't even remember the point of the article, but it made a case for the possibility that whales' language is as sophisticated as ours, very intricate and precise. It also claimed that whale songs travel for hundreds, sometimes thousands of miles in the ocean.

"I was in one of those emotional places where I cursed my entire being. Mad at myself for not looking under the truck, mad at my parents and relatives and teachers for not warning me this kind of pain even exists in the world, mad at God for not looking under *his* truck and seeing me there.

"And I realized I had reached adulthood without even knowing what it is to be human. Nobody ever told me how dangerous it is, how risky. I started wishing I were a whale. At least they know what it *is* to be a whale. I mean, think of it. I walk outside and scream at the top of my lungs, and it travels maybe two blocks. A whale unleashes his cry, and it travels hundreds or even thousands of miles. Every whale in the ocean will at one time or another run into that song. And I figure whales probably don't edit. If they think it, they say it. If some man-whale cheats on his wife, her anguish, her rage, her despair, is heard and understood by every whale who swims into the range of her voice. The joy of lovemaking, the crippling heartache of a lost child—it's all heard and understood. Predators and prey have equal voice. The Mother Teresa whales and the Jeffrey Dahmer whales all have their say. Whale talk is the truth, and in a very short period of time, if you're a whale, you know exactly what it is to be you."

I watch a spider crawl across the ceiling toward the light.

"All that is exactly opposite of what it is to be human, at least for me. My parents were wonderful people, I suppose, but they didn't want me to know what was out there. They didn't want me to know the real skinny on sex or love or boredom or hate or disappointment. They sold me their wishes as if they were fact. After you saw me in the bedroom, I was embarrassed. I feel so *weak* when I get like that. But the truth is, that's just the way it is with me some of the time, and you might as well know it."

I tell him what I haven't said. "I guess I was afraid you were suicidal."

"Suicidal or not, I'm not going to kill myself," he said

with a smile. "If I were going to do that, I'd have done it a long time ago. What you need to know about your old man is that I *always* bounce back."

I went to my room and tried to get some sleep, but I couldn't help running Dad's and my conversation over in my head. If we all spoke in whale talk, and I heard the voices of Chris Coughlin and Andy Mott and Simon DeLong, how would I put them in the same ocean with the shit that comes out of Rich Marshall and Mike Barbour?

By the second round of swim meets we look forward to the road trips as if they are vacations. We have attained a certain celebrity at meets, as Team Bizarro led by Superman. It turns out other teams have a few rookies who probably should have turned out for javelin catching, too, so we pick up unexpected points occasionally, but one coach called us the only team in the state that could actually make a swimming meet last longer. We have learned the trick bad hockey goalies have known forever. When the puck whizzes into the net for the eleventh time in the first period, pretend it didn't happen. If you're Simon or Mott or Jackie Craig, you just pull yourself out of the water as if they weren't waiting for you to get out so they can start the next race. If you're Dan Hole, you leap out, oblivious to all others, hustle to your workout bag, pull out your clipboard and a calculator, and chart your time. If you're Chris Coughlin, you're giddy just to hear your teammates clapping and chanting your name, and if you're Tay-Roy Kibble, you flex as you pull yourself out and the entire crowd forgets why you were in the water in the first place. If you're T. J. Jones, you kick exactly as many asses as dare dive into the water with you.

But the fun is the ride. We study first, then play sports trivia or word games on the trip to the meet, eat pizza and leak out little bits of our lives on the way back. Mott still sits in back listening to his Walkman most of the time, but once in a while he ventures forth to add one scary thing or another, or just listen. I'm gaining more respect for him as I get to know him. The guy has some serious demons, but he keeps them corraled most of the time. Speaking of whale talk, there's a guy who couldn't have known what to expect.

About four weeks from the conference meet our bus lumbers through the night on the way back from Pullman. Coach is sacked out in the seat behind Icko while the rest of us stare out at the carpet of stars laid across the moonless sky on this absolutely clear, subzero night. My father once told me the perspective of an entire generation—and of all generations to follow—changed in late 1968 when the early Apollo astronauts came back with the first pictures of Earth as seen from the moon. "It was the first time most of us knew how *finite* things are here," he said. "A beautiful blue-and-white marble floating in a vast blackness; self-contained and totally dependent upon our care of it. If we poisoned it with our waste, or filled it with dissension and hate, we were pretty much locked in with it. From a physical point of view, God appeared a long ways off."

I keep that picture taped on the inside of my locker at school, and on a poster on the wall in my room at home, alongside another poster of an entire galaxy being born as seen through the eyes of the Hubble telescope, alongside a poster of an atom, because I like to have my mind bent in the way only time and space can bend it. Are we huge or are we small? The distance between the protons and neutrons of a given atom, relative to their size, are as great as the distance between stars. If you were to look at each atom as a universe unto itself, think of the number of universes within each of us; at the same time, look at any one of us in the vast space I am seeing out the window of this bus, which is a molecule on a cell on a flea on a hair on a wart of the *known* universe. And I think of the power, the electricity, that dances between me and Carly, how the emotional part of that, the *connection*, sometimes seems so big it can't be contained. How does that compare with the power of a lightning bolt, or of the nearly silent whisper of a breeze? Are we big or are we small?

"How come none of you guys has ever asked me how I lost my leg?" Mott startles me so bad my forehead bangs against the window.

"Probably because we know you'd tell us to go to hell," I say.

He's quiet, settles into the seat behind me. "Gangrene," he says finally.

I see Icko's eyes in the mirror, penetrating the darkness of the bus.

Dan looks up. "Gracious," he says, "isn't that—"

"Rot," Mott says.

Dan says, "I guess that's one way to express it."

Mott says, "It's the only way to express it."

"Well," Dan says back. "You could always say—"

"Don't say it, Mr. Hole," Icko says. "These aisles are awful damn narrow for push-ups."

"Rot it is," Dan says. He looks at Mott. "How in the world did you contract gangrene?"

"Another time," Mott says. "Hey, Tay-Roy."

"Yeah?"

"You got a picture?"

"Of what?"

"Of you."

"You mean like a school picture?" Tay-Roy asks.

"Naw," Mott says. "I got one of those. Maybe something where you were posin'. You know, like a body contest. Or something out on the river in a tank suit."

"Not with me," Tay-Roy says. "I've got both at home. My mother lives from one Kodak moment to the next. Why?"

"Wanna buy a couple," Mott says.

"What?" Tay-Roy seems confused. "I don't sell pictures of myself."

Mott reaches into his wallet. "Sure you do. You've just never had the opportunity. Give you twenty apiece for them."

Tay-Roy laughs. "Forty bucks for two pictures? Why don't you threaten me, and I'll give them to you free?"

Chris reaches into his wallet, extracts a bent school photo that has to be four years old. "You can have this one," he says. "You can have it for two dollars."

"I got this girlfriend," Mott says to Tay-Roy. "Lives in Birmingham, Alabama."

Tay-Roy says. "That's great. I can't even get one in Cutter."

"Well, you could get one in Birmingham, Alabama," Mott says. "Because I sent this one your picture, and she's dispensing serious drool."

"You sent a girl my picture and told her it was you?"

"Yeah," Mott says. "I scanned your yearbook picture. Told her I'm a bodybuilder, so now I need to scan her some muscles."

"That's crazy," Tay-Roy says. "What will you do when you meet her?"

"She lives in Birmingham, Alabama, for Christ sake," Mott says. "I'm not going to meet her."

"Then what's the point?"

Mott smiles and leans back on the seat, closes his eyes, and simulates whacking off.

Jackie Craig is sitting forward in his seat, completely engrossed and silent as a stifled yawn. Dan is strangely quiet. In the driver's seat, Icko laughs quietly and shakes his head. The lights from an oncoming car highlight Mott's pockmarked cheeks, his hawkish nose. He is not what you'd call classically handsome.

"The Internet is a great equalizer," he says. "A guy can be anybody he wants."

I say, "Yeah, well, so can a girl."

"And the sweeter thing she wants to be, the better I like it," Mott says.

"I don't know if I can go along with this," Tay-Roy says. "Somehow it doesn't seem honest."

"It's not honest," Mott says back. "It's cybersex. Come on, Kibble. If she ever does show up, think of that treat you're in for."

"I don't know," Tay-Roy says. "This kind of thing can backfire."

In a far more timid voice than I've heard him use, Dan says, "I fear it could backfire more times than once."

"Meaning what?" Tay-Roy asks.

"Meaning you are a *Gentleman's Quarterly* item not only in Birmingham, Alabama."

All eyes swing to Dan.

"I'm afraid so," he says. "Evansville, Illinois. I was hoping for something in one of these." He stands and flexes, his fists nearly touching at his belt buckle, imitating a gorilla.

Tay-Roy's eyes widen. "A crab," he says. "Jeez, you guys."

"I'll sign a waiver," Mott tells him.

"I'll draft it right here," Dan says. "If discovered, you can disavow any knowledge. An innocent victim of our lasciviousness."

"That's *it*!" Icko hits the brakes. The aisle is too narrow, but he opens the doors, and Dan racks off ten push-ups in the snow.

"Well worth it," Dan says, "if Tay-Roy yields to our pleas."

Tay-Roy smiles and sighs. "Okay, but if this comes back to bite me, you guys are going to pay." He turns to the others. "Simon, what do you think, you want in on this? Jackie?"

Simon's head shakes in what is almost a vibration. "Naw, I'd probably get confused and send a picture of Mott."

Mott grimaces. "Jesus, a fat kid pretending to be an amputee. Dare to dream."

"You're the new Fabio," I tell Tay-Roy later when everyone else appears to sleep. "Roll with it."

11

It's eleven-thirty when the bus pulls up in front of the school. The parking lot is three-quarters filled with cars of kids attending the aftergame dance, and I decide to check out the action, or, more specifically, to check out Carly. Coach Benson is among the chaperones and meets me at the door.

Benson says, "How'd you guys do?"

"Good," I tell him.

"Everybody hit a personal best?" There is a hint of sarcasm, which I ignore.

"All the way around," I say. "Chris Coughlin took almost fifteen seconds off his four hundred free. Three more meets and we invade Cutter's Crystal Cathedral."

Coach nods and smiles. "Pretty clever how you pulled that off," he says. "Who figured it out, you or your coach?"

"What do you mean?"

"Which one of you figured out everyone would improve this much?"

"Why can't you accept that we gave ourselves a really hard job to do, and did it?"

"I'm going to have a talk with Coach Simet about this," he says. "I have a lot of respect for the athletic program here at Cutter and the excellence of the athletes who succeed."

"I know," I say. "Me, too."

"I wish I thought that were true, Jones." He changes the subject. "So did you take the sprints?"

"Yup."

"Well, I suppose that's the up side to all this. You place high at State and that will put us up in the standings."

"Yeah. That's the problem with sprints, though. No matter how fast you are, some unknown guy hits a perfect dive and turn and takes you out."

"You best concentrate on hitting all your dives and turns," he says. "Things are pretty even around the conference this year, and we're going to need those points. You don't want to be putting the Athletic Council through all this and then come up empty."

I make a mental note to call Simet over the weekend to make sure he knows they're on to us. Benson wields a lot of power around here.

"I'll bust my butt, Coach. I really will. And you have to admit, that's a pretty good trade-off for the rest of these guys earning their jackets. They may not be racking up the points, but I'd die of boredom if they weren't there with me, so they're pulling their weight."

Carly motions to me from across the gym, and I tell Coach I'll catch up with him later.

She says, "I was beginning to think you weren't going to make it."

"Icy roads and a zoo full of swimmers couldn't have kept me away."

She touches my hand, switching on the electricity that has been building between us, and we move onto the dance floor and get lost in the beat of a long slow Celine Dion song. Carly's dark eyes and half smile tease me, and I think how lucky I am to have this uncomplicated relationship with somebody smart to talk to, and hot to the touch. We move closer, eyes closed, feet barely moving, swaying more than dancing. This girl gives me a hummingbird's heart palpitations. I feel her entire body against me, her forehead touching the crook of my neck, the pressure of her hips.

A commotion by the entrance plummets me back to earth, and we look over to see Kristen Sweetwater jerking her wrist out of Mike Barbour's grip, yelling, "Leave me alone, you asshole!" Kristen is the head varsity cheerleader and one of Carly's good friends.

Carly drops my hand, and I follow her toward them. She says, "I told her to stay away from him."

Barbour glances at the staring crowd and releases Kristen. "Come on, goddamn it, let's talk about it."

"You bastard, Mike Barbour! Look at my arm! Get away from me!" That is *not* language you hear out of Kristen Sweetwater.

Coach Benson hustles toward them, but Barbour sees him and storms out.

Kristen drops to her butt on the bleachers, face in her hands, sobbing. Carly sits beside her and puts an arm around her shoulders, waving Benson away and firing threatening looks at anyone who approaches. "What happened?"

Kristen doesn't answer, just shakes her head and cries harder.

"Kristen, what *happened*? Did he hurt you?"

She pulls the loose sleeve of her blouse up to her shoulder. Her entire arm is red, beginning to darken.

"That son of a bitch," Carly says.

"He said he had some beer stashed out by the river," she

said. "He and some friends were supposed to have a little party out there."

"Only you got out there and no one else was there. Shit, Kristen, what's the matter with you? I told you what Mike Barbour is like."

Kristen looks up, wiping her eyes. I haven't said anything because I can't take my eyes off her arm. "Yeah, well," she says, "that's what got me in trouble. When I saw we were alone, I told him you said he was like that, and he started getting *mad*. He said if I was going to listen to some bitch who's fu—going out with a ni—who's going out with T. J., he didn't want anything to do with me."

Carly massages Kristen's neck. "That would have been a good time to tell him to take you home."

Kristen's head drops. "I know."

"But you didn't say that, did you?"

Kristen is defeated. "No. I told him I didn't necessarily believe it, just that you'd said it. Then he said I could make it up to him by having sex. I thought he was kidding—I mean, I've only been out with him a couple of times—but all of a sudden he was unbuttoning my coat and I was trying to get out and accidentally scratched his face. God, he went crazy. He kept telling me to strip, and I'd say no and he'd punch my arm." She starts crying again, hard. "And he had me trapped, and he said, 'Strip' again, and I said no and he punched my arm again, then he just kept saying it faster and faster and hitting me before I could answer." Her voice trails away into sobs.

I am pulling my coat on.

Carly says, "Wait, T. J."

Kristen is gasping for breath. "I finally jerked loose and started running. He started his pickup and came after me,

141

but Don Abernathy and Marcy Caldwell saw me and stopped. I had them bring me back here, but Mike followed us."

She catches her breath. "God, I am so *stupid*! He stopped me after I got out of their car and said he was sorry, that he's really been under a lot of pressure and would I at least get back in the pickup with him and talk about it."

Carly's eyes harden. "And you did it. Jesus, Kristen."

"I know, but he sounded really sorry. And he was. When I first got in, he looked at my arm and apologized again and said he'd never lay another hand on me, that he'd do anything not to have done that. He sounded like he was going to cry and so I was kind of holding him and all of a sudden he was feeling me up again. I jumped out, and that's when he followed me in."

I tap Carly's shoulder. "Okay, I waited. Now I'm going to find Barbour."

"T. J., don't do something stupid."

"I won't. I'm going to kick his ass," I say and head for the door.

"T. J.!"

"You guys wait here for me. I'll be right back." I am through the exit, ignoring the sophomore money-taker reminding me I need a chaperone's permission to leave if I want back in.

I don't see Barbour's pickup in the lot, which is packed now, and I jog up one aisle and down the next, working myself up. If I find him, that pickup is scrap metal. "Barbour! Come out, big man! Let's see how tough you are! Here's your chance, tough guy! You been saying 'someday'! Well, it's here! Barbour!"

Headlights flash on as I pass cars—I'll probably have to

issue a class-action apology for all the near misses I caused—and then I hear an engine roar and look up to see Barbour fishtailing out the entrance. If somebody clocked me, I might have the new school record for the hundred meters between me and my car.

I hit the parking-lot exit at top speed for a Chevy Corvair in second gear, which barely approaches the speed limit, and gun it down the street, only slowing enough at intersections to look for him. I will run that son of a bitch off the road if necessary; we are going to deal before I go to sleep tonight.

The speeding/failure-to-stop citation is going to cost me $273 even though I pass the Breathalyzer. The cop says if I get another one tonight he will see that I spend the rest of it in jail, because I am so pissed I can't keep my mouth shut while he's writing it out. "I suggest you go home and cool off," he tells me.

"That asshole punches out a girl, and *I'm* the one going to jail."

"Tell her to report it," he says. "If it happened like you say, it's assault."

"It happened like I say."

"Well, if there are bruises, she's got a case."

"She won't report it."

"Hey, buddy. If she won't report it, as far as the law's concerned, it didn't happen."

I take the ticket and thank him through clenched teeth.

"Look, Mr. Jones," he says, reading my driver's license as he hands it back. "Go home. The guy who throws the first punch never gets the foul. It's the guy the ref sees retaliate. You're close enough to eighteen to go straight to the slammer."

143

As I pull back onto the street, he follows me: my designated escort. I can forget evasive action; my address is on the ticket. Fine. Barbour will live an extra day. This shit *will* get cleaned up.

I pull over and, when the cop stops behind me, get out to ask if I can go back to the dance to hook up with Kristen and Carly. He points straight ahead. "Home."

It's quarter to one when I find Mom in her study going over papers for a case she has to try Monday morning. I show her the ticket.

"Were you running from Carly's dad?" My mom can be a smartass, too.

I tell her about Kristen's shoulder; that I was going after Barbour.

"So what were you going to do if you found him?"

"You mean, what *am* I going to do."

In the voice she reserves for hostile witnesses, she says, "No, I mean what *were* you going to do—before you let your temper get you a ticket equal to a semester's tuition."

"Mom, somebody's got to teach that asshole he can't be doing that. He gets some bullshit in his head and takes it out on some girl maybe half his size? What kind of ignorant shit is that?"

"Just that," she says. "Ignorant shit."

"Yeah, well, he needs a lesson."

"And you're going to teach it?"

"Damn right. If I'd have found him tonight it would be in the record books."

"If you had found him tonight, there's a good chance your dad would be down at the county jail right now, bailing you out. Jail, T. J., not juvy; because you're that close to eighteen, just like the officer told you. And then who would pay your brand-new giant-sized car insurance premium?"

144

"You think the law wouldn't give me a flyer on this one? He hit a girl so hard her shoulder is going to be *black*. What about that? Isn't that evidence?"

She pushes her chair back from the desk, closes the folder, and sighs, which means I'm about to get hit with lawyer shit. "Yes, T. J., it is evidence. It's evidence against Mike Barbour for an assault he'll never be charged with, because the person he hit will say it was accidental after he apologizes and swears never to do it again, which"—and she glances at her watch—"he probably has already done, and she won't go through with it because it will prove to her, in some perverse way, that she isn't good enough to keep him." She leans forward to make her point. "It won't even come up in *your* assault trial."

"So I just let it happen?"

"No. Kristen Sweetwater lets it happen."

"What the hell is she supposed to do? She weighs maybe a hundred-ten pounds."

"What would Carly do?"

"She'd kick his ass."

"No, she'd stay away from him."

I slam my fist into my open hand so hard it almost goes numb. "Something's got to be done, and if no one else will do it, I will." I start to walk out of the den, but Mom's firm hand grips my shoulder and guides me back to the chair. She says, "Sit."

I sit.

"As long as we're going down this road, let's go all the way. What is it you think you're going to teach Mike Barbour by beating him up?"

"To pick on somebody his own size."

"It seems to me that if you beat him up you'll be teaching him *not* to pick on somebody his own size."

"You know what I mean."

"I know what you think you mean."

"Are you going to do this lawyer thing with me?"

"This *lawyer thing* is common sense. How do you think Mike Barbour got like he is? Or Rich Marshall for that matter?" It sounds like Mom has been talking to Dad.

"I don't care how they got that way. I'm just tired of them thinking they're big men because they can beat up on girls and little kids."

"Do you really believe they think they're big men because they do that?"

"Why else would they do it?"

She places a hand on my knee. "You're not going to like this, but for the same reason you break things in your room sometimes, or punch your hand so hard it sounds like you broke your fingers. Because when rage takes you over, you do what the rage tells you."

"Hey, I might break stuff, but I sure don't hit women and kids."

"And don't think I'm not grateful," she says, only half kidding. I know she's right about my rage, but I'm *not* giving that asshole Barbour even an inch.

"What do you think Mike Barbour does when he goes home after doing something like he did tonight? Do you really think he goes into the bathroom and looks in the mirror and flexes his biceps and says, 'Well, I really kicked *her* ass'?"

"I don't know what he does."

"So I'll tell you. He feels out of control. He promises himself he won't do it again, worries what will happen to him. He worries somebody will find out and humiliate him. He wishes he knew why he doesn't stop himself, why he didn't see it coming. None of that lasts long, because he

146

has to find some way to justify it, so he starts telling himself what a bitch Kristen is, that it's her job to keep him from getting mad. And I'll tell you what, I don't even know Kristen Sweetwater, but I'll bet you the price of that ticket that she was brought up by a father who believes exactly what Mike Barbour believes."

This is probably why my mother is such a hell of a lawyer; she actually makes me stop and think, when all I wanted a few minutes ago was blood.

"You don't remember, T. J., but if you don't believe this, ask Georgia: When you came to us, you were *inconsolable*. Your mother had left you alone for days. You had diaper rash so bad your butt looked like a crater. And thrush, my God. You'd been left unattended for hours on end, sometimes days. You ate when your mother felt hungry, which was the only time she was reminded that you might be hungry, too, and she was eating darn little, because she was *launched* on meth.

"Your dad and I fed you and cleaned you up and held you and walked the floor till we were both blind with exhaustion, and nothing quieted you. The day your mother came to say good-bye, she walked through the door, and you stopped crying the instant you saw her. She held you and cried, and you didn't utter a peep. Not a *peep*. Within seconds of her leaving, you cranked up again."

"The point being—" I'd heard that story before.

"That you didn't respond to what was good for you, you responded to what you knew, what was familiar. That's what Mike Barbour does, and Rich. That's what Kristen Sweetwater does. And if you think you're going to teach anyone a lesson, get ready to learn one yourself.

"Georgia came and let you rage; let you play out every

trauma. One day you'd be the helpless, thumb-sucking victim, the next you'd kick the hell out of anything that got in
your way. Over and over and over you played out your life,
until finally you had done it all enough to feel at some
primitive level like you had it under control. I'm not kidding, T. J.; it went on for nine months. That's how you
learned. You played it out and played it out. If we hadn't
had Georgia, I wouldn't have known *what* to do. But I
know this: I'd have decided enough was enough long before
it was enough for you, and I would have put a stop to it.
And according to Georgia, that would have set the fear and
rage so deep in you it might not ever have come out."

I'm drifting off in my room, maybe a half hour later, visions
of punching Mike Barbour's chest so hard his heart stops
dancing in my head, when the light comes on.

"Hey, big boy." It's Dad.

I squint into the light. "Is there a fire?"

He laughs. "No fire. I've been talking with your mom."

"So you know about Barbour."

"Guess we shouldn't be surprised," he says, "as much as
he hangs out with Rich Marshall."

"Yeah, they've got a real mentoring system going there."

"Your mom says you were so mad you were getting
ready to commit a crime."

"I was just going to kick his ass."

"Yeah, that's what I meant."

"I do not get what is such a big deal about a fight," I tell
him. "I mean, if someone were threatening Mom, you'd do
whatever you had to do to stop him."

"You're right. And if you had been there when Rich was
hurting that girl, I'd have expected you to do whatever you
had to do to stop it."

148

"Ah, so this is about timing."

"This is about 'what's done is done.' Look, the Mike Barbours and Rich Marshalls of the world have just as much right to exist as you do. They have just as much purpose. You think it's your job to teach them a lesson, but they're not going to learn any lesson you're going to teach, so I have a feeling it's the other way around. You kick Mike Barbour's ass, and it just cranks him up to be more like he already is. He'll immediately turn it racial and respond by hurting somebody else. He and Marshall both have that amazing capacity to believe that other people make us do things."

"Dad, that's great philosophy, but what about Kristen Sweetwater?"

"What is Kristen Sweetwater going to get out of you wasting Barbour?"

"Revenge."

"Exactly. She's not going to learn one thing about standing on her own two feet. She'll learn she has power only when you or Carly is around."

"So I just let guys like Barbour do their thing."

"You can't keep guys like Barbour from doing their thing. Look, T. J., if you were going to teach Heidi to stay away from mean dogs, would you go out and find one mean dog and teach her all about him? Or would you show her as many mean dogs as you could find, and tell her about the ones you couldn't find?"

"Yeah, but—"

"And if a mean dog attacked her, would you beat hell out of it and let her around it again?"

"No, Dad, but somebody would put it down."

"Right. Somebody would kill it. But we're not going to kill Mike Barbour, and nothing short of that is going to change the way he treats people."

I am *so* goddamned exasperated.

"Look, T. J. Your mother and I have been in court on these kinds of cases almost as long as you've been alive. Me as a Guardian ad Litem and her as a lawyer. We see it over and over. You know what Mike Barbour's like. No way is this the first time he tried to strong-arm that girl. And I'll bet you the price of any of my classic cycles you want that she's been in this same spot with other guys. Now, you protect people in the moment they need protection, or ahead of time. But not after. After, you work with them."

He watches me, and I watch the ceiling.

"What can I do to help, son?"

"I don't know. Rich Marshall and Barbour or guys like them have been in my life as long as I can remember. I don't invite them in, but they're always there. I'm sick of 'em."

"They're there for a reason," he says. "When you figure out what it is, you won't even notice them anymore."

"I guess I *did* invite Barbour in when I entered the war over the letter jackets."

"Focus on that, then—the jock stuff. At least you're taking Barbour on in your own life instead of someone else's. Those swimmers, they're your friends. You guys are into something together there. You can do the letter jacket thing without even talking to Barbour or Marshall. Do your best, win the letter, and wear it with pride."

It's not bad advice, and I'm so tired I think my eyes are going to bleed, so I say good night to Dad and banish him from my room. As he steps through the door to leave, I say, "Dad?"

"Yeah?"

"You should have been a whale."

12

If I am going to accept the Rich Marshalls and Mike Barbours of the world, I have to accept that it won't be mutual. Big duh. The longer Heidi stays at our place, the more rattled Rich gets and the better look I get at him. The four weekends in jail he received for showing up at our place bearing arms are *not* rehabilitating him, and he has not taken his suspension from duties as Cutter's returning jock savior lightly. My mother did as promised. The day after his midnight visit, she marched into Morgan's office and told him if Rich Marshall set foot on the grounds while school was in session, Morgan had damned well better polish his witness stand persona because she would keep him up there until he was old and sorry. Let me tell you, my mother can turn from a protector of the young into the kind of lawyer everyone makes vicious jokes about in the time it takes Simon DeLong to eat a box of marshmallow-covered Snowballs, so even though Morgan tried to minimize Rich's actions, he doesn't dare let him back onto the premises.

So Morgan calls me into the office on Tuesday of the week after my record-setting speeding ticket. Coach Benson is there, and my thoughts fly immediately to a future article in *The Wolverine*, exposing what I fear will be the Athletic Inquisition.

Morgan says, "T. J., I want you to know this is off the record."

I ask if that means I can cuss.

"I suppose, if you feel the need," he says. Morgan missed the humor class when he went to principal school. Benson was absent that day, too.

I promise to keep myself under control.

"I've heard rumors."

I glance to Benson, but can read nothing.

"That something is brewing between you and Mike Barbour."

"That's not a rumor, that's the way of the world."

"So you admit it's true."

"Things have been brewing between me and Mike Barbour since we started high school," I tell him. "I'll do my best to see they don't come to a boil just yet."

"Is this about the letter jackets?"

I quote my mother. "It's about dead baby deer and sports and girlfriends and your basic struggle between good and evil," I say. "Nothing that can't wait until five or ten minutes after graduation."

"Coach Benson tells me there was trouble at the dance the other night."

"There could have been, but there wasn't; other than that I may be paying my own car insurance."

Benson says, "I'd like to know what that was all about, T. J."

"It was about your star defensive back hammering on a girl," I tell him. "It's a good thing my parents got to me before I got to him, Coach."

"There are two sides to every story, T. J. That's not exactly the way Mike tells it."

"How many guys do you know who beat on their girl-friends and then come out and say so?"

"Mike tells that a little differently. And they're back together."

Shit. "It must be tough being an educator; having to figure out who to believe all the time. I know!" I say sarcastically. "Why don't we go have a look at Kristen Sweetwater's arm."

"Don't get smart with me, T. J."

I turn to Morgan. "I thought this was off the record." Then back to Coach. "Don't worry, nothing will come of it. Your golden boy will graduate to O. J. status before you know it. Look, why am I here?"

"Mike Barbour has a full ride to the U. I think he has a pretty good chance to be successful there. I don't want this ballooning into something bigger than it is. I'm just protecting his reputation. You have to admit, T. J., you can be pretty dramatic. I can't help but remember that bloody shirt you wore to school for a full week, then brought in your parents to block the school from holding you responsible."

"I can't help but remember how it got bloody."

"Maybe. But you and Rich Marshall tell a different story there, too."

"So you're worried about me soiling Barbour's rep, huh? Well, everything from here on out is on the up-and-up. No dramatics, and my swimming guys won't be wearing T-shirts with a picture of Mike Barbour under a red circle with a slash through it. We'll be wearing letter jackets. No slanderous remarks. Barbour will last long enough in college to beat up plenty of girls."

About ninety-eight percent of the time, Benson is Don

Shula. The other two percent, he's Bobby Knight. I've seen him blow on the football field a couple of times, and he can be truly scary. His face reddens like a thermometer in a blast furnace and the vein in his neck swells up like a miniature python. I see the reptile in him coming out this minute.

"By God, Jones, if you were eighteen, that statement would be libelous, and I'd encourage Mike Barbour to pursue it. I've kept my mouth shut about you for four years, watched you waste athletic talent most boys would kill for, flaunt your skills at Hoopfest or playing flag football games, and doing not one damn thing for your school. Well, you've pretty much ruined a career before it could get started, but I'll be damned if I'll watch you drag other athletes down with you. This charade you and your coach are pulling to get your band of nobodies into letter jackets is *not* going to happen if I have anything to say about it."

"You already had something to say about it, Coach," I say. "The Athletic Council already voted. It was unanimous."

"It was unanimous because no one knew what you were up to," he says. "It can be brought back for a vote."

The trick to being a good smartass is knowing when to call it good, and I figure now is about right for me to take my leave. It always feels better to let the *other* guy get mad—a sensation I don't get to have too often. "So, am I out of here, then? No assault rumors against Barbour, no subversive articles about the football team on steroids?"

Morgan says, "Yeah, Mr. Jones, you're out of here."

I'm in Simet's room before Morgan's door slams. "Benson wants another Athletic Council vote on our letters," I say. Man, the last thing I want is for my guys to miss out on

154

their jackets. Points and wins have been scarce and non-existent in that order. The jacket remains the prize.

"Don't worry about it," Simet says. "When this whole thing started, I was a little skeptical about your plan to get Our Gang into letter jackets. But there isn't another group of jocks in this school that works as hard as we do. The wrestling team would come closest, but even they have some slackers. Our guys put out every minute of every workout. I've never coached a team like this before. There isn't a kid out there who doesn't deserve a letter."

"Yeah, but Benson is going to argue that we pulled the wool over the council's eyes. He's pissed, Coach."

"Then I'll be pissed, too. It's all relative, like anything else. If we keep this team together after you're gone, the requirements will get stiffer, plus this 'better on every swim' thing is finite. This was a good call." He gets a firm grip on my shoulder. "And by the way, anything you hear in this room stays in this room, right?"

"Hey, I've signed a confidentiality oath," I tell him. "Course, I might have to charge you."

When I get home from school, we have a new houseguest, and Heidi is beside herself with glee. My mother and Georgia and the caseworker have put their heads together and decided it's best to put Alicia in foster care along with Heidi. That way she can't make decisions that will put Heidi in danger and Heidi doesn't have to lose her. Of course, that also means we have her twins. Alicia has sworn she won't tell Rich she's here, and she knows if she does anything to put the kids in his care, she goes and the kids stay.

Dad tells me we are going to implement the Marshall

Plan, which, if you know your American history, is a pretty good pun. Our Marshall Plan is simple. If you see Rich, or if he calls the house, dial 911. There is a restraining order on him for Alicia and the kids, as well as for us. "If I know Rich Marshall," he says, "he'll know where everyone is by this time tomorrow night. Whether he comes around depends on how much jail time he wants to log."

It's a pretty wild evening, with Heidi so glad to see her mother and all three kids fighting for Alicia's time while her fuse smolders and she tries not to blow up at them in front of my parents. Mom seems to understand she's on a short leash and helps with Heidi, while Dad distracts the boys, who I call Thing One and Thing Two. This is probably the first time Heidi's been in a house with her mother and brothers where she's been afforded equal footing, and she's taking full advantage. By the time the kids are in bed, Alicia looks exhausted, and she steps out onto the front porch for a cigarette. I see her standing there, back to the door, a curl of smoke winding its way lazily toward the porch light. I pull on my coat and step out, dusting the skiff of snow off the porch swing to sit.

"Hey."

She doesn't turn. "Hey."

"Guess we're going to be family here for a while."

"I guess." She sounds cold, protected. "You okay with it?"

"Sure. Why wouldn't I be?"

She still doesn't turn around. "You know, Rich and all. Heidi."

I say, "Heidi and I are tight."

"I know, T. J. That's my point." She sounds irritated.

"Could I ask you something?"

"You can *ask*."

"What keeps you with a guy like Rich?"

She is quiet.

"I mean, you don't love him, right?"

"What do you know about love? You're a kid."

"Yeah, Alicia. I'm maybe five or six years younger than you."

She takes a drag on the cigarette and finally turns to face me. In many ways, she's a lot more than five or six years older than me. She says, "You must hate me."

"I don't hate you. I just don't get it about Rich, and about Heidi."

"I don't either, T. J. I know what they say in my therapy groups, and what my counselor says. They say I feel worthless, and I have to prove the things to him that I could never prove to my dad. They say I have an overwhelming need for approval, and all he has to do to keep me around is not approve. They say I tell myself he cares about me because he wouldn't get that mad at someone he doesn't care about. They say the only way I think I can get power is to let him hurt me so he'll come crawling back, begging me not to leave." Alicia flicks the cigarette out into the snow.

I ask how much of that is true.

"All of it. But knowing it and doing something about it are two different things. I'm hoping living here will make the difference. I want to quiet my insides, get back to some feeling I can tolerate." She sighs. "I guess some girls don't feel complete unless they have two assholes."

I watch her; listen. Under those hard times on her face, she's a really pretty woman, and she has to be smart or she couldn't have laid all that out for me. That makes it harder to understand.

"I just can't be with anybody, that's all." She pauses,

157

shaking her head slowly. "It was different with Willis, Heidi's dad." She chokes a second, remembering. "I mean, he was good to me but he could keep me interested." She pauses again. "But then he was gone and I came back to Rich, and except for the fact that Rich won't let me forget that I slept with a ni—Willis, it's like he never existed, like maybe I dreamed it."

"There's Heidi."

She looks me in the eye. "Things are going to get bad around here, T. J. I told your parents that. Rich will find me whether I let him know where I am or not; he always does. And you need to know he *really* hates you. He's accused me of fucking you. He's accused you of trying to take Heidi away from him. He *hates* that I've been with a black man, and his worst fear is that I want to be with another one. That's the one thing he'll never forgive me for. You want to watch out for him. You see only the very tip of what's going on with him."

I tell her thanks for the warning.

"Well, let me give you one more. I'm going to try to make it work here, I really am. I feel strong right now, but I know how I am. When the stars line up right, I'll lie and protect him and deny this conversation ever took place."

Man, this shit makes absolutely no sense, but all I have to do to believe her is look in her eyes. "That must drive you crazy."

She looks at me like "No shit."

We talk a little about Kristen Sweetwater, and she says about what my parents said. "It doesn't matter who you are. You can be a pretty little cheerleader who looks like she owns the world, or you can be that funky little guy on your swim team that Mike hates so much, or you can be me. Deal is, if you've been treated bad, you're going to have to find a way to get over it."

I ask how she knows about Chris.

"Are you kidding? Mike hangs out with Rich all the time. Half of what they talk about is how things are going to hell at Cutter High. I swear, if I'm ever going to get over Rich, it will be because he's dumber than dirt. Who cares about a high school football team?"

By the time we get to the conference meet, which is held at Frost High School in Spokane this year, all of us are pretty much assured of lettering if the Athletic Council doesn't do a recall vote. Simet says it would be close anyway. A couple of the girls' coaches would vote our way, and several votes are up in the air. Anyway, it will be the last meet for everyone but me, and we've tapered off our workouts, so times are dropping like rocks. Actually, I'm the only one who came close to not making it. In the second to last dual meet I almost missed my turn in the fifty, had to haul serious ass to get back, and, in fact, bettered my time by only a hundredth of a second. Coach isn't going to swim anyone but me in that event at conference, because it's too easy to miss a turn or get off the blocks slow and wreck your chances, and my time already qualifies me for State.

By now the coaches in the other sports are behind me a hundred percent, Benson included, because if I pull out a couple of top three finishes in the sprints and even as low as sixth in the two hundred, we'll have serious pointage toward the all-sport championship, and the school who gets that has major bragging rights. Cutter has never won it because we've always been big in the major sports but have fallen down in sports like gymnastics and soccer and cross-country. And, of course, we've never had a swim team before.

On Friday morning the student body gathers on the school lawn, complete with the cheerleaders lined up on the steps like Rockettes, as Icko brings the bus around, and though no one is going to watch us swim, they cheer as if we're the football team. Mott is on the bus already, having stopped Icko as he came through the parking lot. Chris stands totally amazed, waving at the crowd, while Jackie simply watches, not embarrassed, not anything that I can see. I see Tay-Roy tap Kristen on the shoulder before coming down to join us, and as we stand there ready to board, I elbow him. "Kristen Sweetwater?"

He looks embarrassed but keeps smiling. That would be *so* sweet.

"She's cool," I whisper, "but what are you going to tell your girls in Birmingham? And Evanston?"

Dan Hole is so busy calculating the times he should hit, he is oblivious to the celebration. Barbour and some of the football guys stand together to one side; only a few of them clap or cheer because he has convinced them this whole thing is a ploy to diminish their standing as nobility at Cutter High. The jock wars continue.

Carly moves quickly through the crowd to my side. "You sure you don't want me to come see this?" she asks. "You've never missed one of my games."

"I'll tell you again what I tell my parents," I say. "On the boredom scale, watching a swim meet is one step below watching mold grow. Come see me at Hoopfest."

She says, "Come see *me* at Hoopfest." And I say, "Will do."

* * *

160

The bleachers at the conference pool at Frost are packed; swimming is a much bigger thing among schools with swimming history. There's only one guy in our conference who can challenge me in the sprints when I'm at my best, and that's Scott Wakefield from Frost. He's within a tenth of me in the fifty and two-tenths in the hundred. A couple of guys have slightly better times than mine in the two hundred. The big sprinters are on the coast, around Tacoma and Seattle. The fifty at State would look like a six-way dead heat if it weren't for the electronic touchpads, but over here Wakefield and I should blow the field away. I'm gaining a bit of celebrity on our side of the state, partly because of the number of black swimmers any of them have seen, and partly because it's by now well known what our training facility looks like. The Spokane and Wenatchee coaches have already approached me to swim on their summer teams—they think I could actually make the Olympic trials down the road, with proper training—but I'm pretty sure this will be my last season in the water. Spring is around the corner, and I'm antsy to resume honing my basketball skills for Hoopfest. I believe there are no black swimmers in the swimming hall of fame because swimming is no damn fun.

We are not prepared for Chris's response to crowds. He's been gathering confidence every time he touches the wall and sees his time is faster than the last, which, by the way, speaks to his ability to learn, because he knows the *second* he sees it. The swimmers on the other teams know his story now and always cheer him on. This kid hits times that would win fourth place in the 11–12 age group of a novice meet, and every time he finishes, the crowd erupts. He has taken to blowing kisses toward the cheers.

161

He and Mott are entered in the five hundred freestyle, and the entire team from Moses Lake chants his name as he steps onto the block. He turns and waves, smiling wide and basking in the glow as the starting gun fires. The crowd screams, "Go!"—which confuses him, and he watches in bewilderment as the field pulls away. Jackie has the presence of mind to run over and push him in, which should technically disqualify Chris, but the judges give us leeway, and once he hits the water, instinct takes over and his arms rotate like propellers. Adrenaline alone puts him back on pace for his best time at a hundred-fifty yards, and when he sees his time at the finish, he squeals. His opponents have passed the word not to get out of the water before any of our guys finish, and though it's only a prelim, they all duck under their lane ropes to congratulate him. Something about the entire experience makes me like these guys a lot.

The rest of the meet is uneventful. I lose the fifty by a hair, but I didn't get the best start, so I'm not worried, and I win the hundred by almost a half body length. I finish third in the two hundred, and we climb on to the bus in the late Saturday afternoon darkness with the best meet of our lives under our belts.

We get our traditional pizza to go, and soon we're on the highway, having entered our mermen's cocoon for what we believe is the last time. The school won't fund any of the other guys to go along with Simet and me to State. We get mileage for Simet's Humvee, a double room at Motel 6, and per diem of fifteen bucks a day each. The football team stayed at the Doubletree.

As we roll over bare roads through the cold, clear night, Simet stands next to Icko, facing us, holding tight to the bar by the door. He says, "Guys, I've been with some good teams in my time. My AAU team took fifteen swimmers to

Nationals when I was sixteen, and several of us made it to the NAIA finals my junior and senior years in college. But I've never had an athletic experience like this one. I've never swum on or coached a team where not one swimmer backed off on even one repeat. I know there's been controversy over whether or not you guys should letter, but most of that controversy is being caused by guys who couldn't carry your jocks, if you had any. There is not an athlete at Cutter who has more right to wear the blue and gold than the guys on this bus."

"Fuckin' A," Mott says from the back of the bus.

"Fuckin' A," Coach says right back at him.

"Fuckin' A," Chris Coughlin says, and covers his mouth.

Mott waits a few minutes, then sneaks up into the seat behind me. "You gonna go over there and make us look good, hotshot?" he says.

"Do my best."

"The muscle man says we got to swim relays against you for the next couple of weeks. That right?"

"You guys don't have to do that. You kept me going all this time. It'd be shitty to make you stretch out another two weeks when you don't even get to swim."

Tay-Roy says, "No, man, this is a *team*. Our season lasts as long as one of us is still alive."

"Yeah, but—"

"Look at it this way," Mott says. "We get two more weeks free membership at All Night."

"Yeah, but—"

Simet says, "It's done, T. J. Shut up."

I do.

It's quiet a few more miles. In a low voice, Mott says, "How come you guys never asked me about my gangrene?"

"Same reason we didn't ask you about your leg in the first place," Tay-Roy says. "Jeez, Mott, don't you know your own rep?"

"I'm granting serial killer's dispensation," Mott says.

Chris says, "You gots a green gang? What's that?"

"Fuck," Mott says. "We've gotta keep this team together just to keep that boy out of an institution." He says it low enough that Chris doesn't hear. "Somebody tell him what gangrene is."

"Rot," Dan says, "pure and simple."

Icko says, "Last meet of the year, and the boy genius finally utters a one-syllable word all on his own."

We sit through a few more seconds of silence. Even when Mott feels like talking, he does it at his own pace.

"You guys know a guy named Rance Haskins?"

Everyone knows Rance Haskins. About four years ago he killed an eighteen-month-old infant by squeezing his stomach because he peed his pants. The Department of Social and Health Services took a *lot* of heat because the mother's relatives had lined up with complaints that he was dangerous, warning that they couldn't get the baby's mother away from him. Rance got three years for involuntary manslaughter, was out in a year and a half, then blinded a second child by shaking her. The mother of the blinded baby wouldn't testify against him, so he ended up back in the slammer for parole violation, because he wasn't supposed to be around children. The guy did in two kids and was out of prison in three years and a month. Free and clear. Rance Haskins is a famous guy. The Spokane newspaper does a story on him every once in a while.

"I don't know him," I say. "But I know who he is."

"Well, before he was famous, he was my mom's boy-friend."

164

I'm not going to like this story.

"My old lady didn't have any excuses. She didn't take drugs, didn't drink; hell, she wouldn't even take an aspirin. Rance made her dance at the Déjà Vu in Spokane for extra cash. She looked pretty good for somebody took as much shit as she did. She'd want to take me to work with her, but the bosses wouldn't allow it, and Rance wouldn't let her use her own damn money to put me in day care when he considered himself a perfectly good baby-sitter. Man, if you want to pass up purgatory and go straight to hell, you want to enroll in Rance Haskins's Day Care. Soon as my mom would take off for work, he'd tie my leg to the pipe under the kitchen sink, give me a big ol' aluminum bowl to pee in, and take off with his buddies, or invite them over for a little drugfest. Got so messed up this one time, he passed out and his friends hauled him off to Emergency. My old lady just happened to go home from Déjà Vu with some guy to pick up some extra cash, and I'd been there almost twenty-four hours. I guess I kept trying to get away, but ol' Rance was a real Boy Scout, and the knot just got tighter. Time Mom found me, my foot was discolored all the way up my calf. Gangrene set in, and in the end they had to whack that baby off before it snuck up and got something really important."

Chris Coughlin leans forward in his seat, his eyes glued to Mott's silhouette outlined in the side window. Brothers in arms.

"Jesus, Mott," I say. "What did the doctors say when they saw your leg?"

"Haskins is a smart cookie. Took me to this hometown doc in Baxter Falls, little town about twenty miles outside of nowhere. Made up some cock-and-bull story the guy believed. Then we moved to Oregon for a couple of years,

165

so when the people there saw me, I was already a one-legged kid. That's when he left her. Came back up here and got famous."

"Who else knows this?"

"Me. You guys."

"How come you never told?"

He shrugs. "Hell, I barely remember it, don't know if I really do. Rance is gone. Leg's gone. Who do you tell? Got damn fast on crutches. My mother blackmailed Rance into puttin' hard-earned drug money into a trust fund so I could get this space-age leg soon as I finished growing. No point telling anyone now."

I start to ask why he's telling us, but I know. It's a gift.

"An' you guys don't tell nobody either, got it?"

"Jeez, Mott, don't you want to get him?"

"Guys like Rance Haskins already been got," Mott says. "Hell, he doesn't care if he spends the rest of his life in prison or in Palm Springs. He's the same miserable son of a bitch no matter where he is."

"Maybe, but Jesus, Mott. He got your leg."

Mott brings his leg up on the seat, raises the leg of his sweatpants. "Yeah, but look what he left me. This baby's bionic."

Simet and Icko are doing what they always do during these conversations, remaining invisible unless we invite them in. God, what must Coach be thinking? Here are these guys, brought into his sphere of influence under the guise of a swim team that can't swim. For some of them, he and Icko are the only decent adults they've ever known. There's nothing he can do about the past for any of them. And now the only thing he can do about the present is stand up for them against the rest of the Athletic Council,

166

who want to rob them of their letter jackets. I'm proud of what we've accomplished. I felt tremendous relief today when Jackie Craig and Simon DeLong finished the hundred-yard backstroke in personal bests, because it meant everyone had safely lettered, that we'd accomplished our goal, or at least *my* goal. I know the whole thing is only symbolic, a gesture. But it's a hell of a gesture, because it lets us stand up for ourselves in the language that is understood at this school. Part of me doesn't want it to end, because it's so much more than what I had in mind in the beginning, and I don't know if what we got from it can ever be re-created.

13

The monthly Athletic Council meeting is set for lunchtime of the Monday we return from the conference meet. I get a note from Simet between first and second periods to see him in his room before he goes in. "These guys must have stayed up late," he says. "They're pushing hard to revote on our letter requirements. I told 'em I was bringing you with me."

"Bet they loved that."

"Everything's relative. I threatened to bring the whole team. I think Andy Mott makes everyone nervous."

"Mott is my personal hero."

"Benson is bringing some representatives from the football team, and I guess Roundtree is bringing a couple of hoopsters. There is some common feeling that I misrepresented the truth." He laughs.

"What do you want me to say?"

"I just want you there to have us represented. You may not have to say anything. Play it by ear, but whatever you do, don't lose your temper and don't get into it with Barbour. It could be a tight vote, and you don't want to piss anyone off."

I run into Carly coming out of Simet's room and bring her up to speed. "This is too cool," she says. "Janet Lindstrom is the girls' sports rep to the council, and she's gone. I'm first alternate. I don't know how Janet would vote, but

I'm in your pocket, if you play your cards right." She kisses me on the cheek. God, I love her. She is so perfect for me, requires so little.

Simet and I walk into the council a few minutes late because of a last-minute strategy meeting, and the room falls silent, making me wonder if Benson and Roundtree had a last-minute strategy meeting of their own.

Benson is chairperson for the year, and as he opens the meeting, I realize if parliamentary rules are in play he can vote only in case of a tie, so between that and the addition of Carly, we may have been handed a two-vote swing. He dispatches with old business in about fifteen seconds, then calls for new.

Mike Barbour raises his hand. "I move to call for a review on the letter requirements for the swim team."

Before anyone can respond, Carly says, "Call for discussion."

There is agreement.

Barbour says, "The letter requirements were misrepresented to the council, I believe."

That's *way* more articulate than Barbour is. Somebody has been coaching him to imitate a human.

Simet knows how to play this game. "Misrepresented? You're saying I deceived you?" He turns to Barbour. "That's the gentleman's way of saying 'You callin' me a liar?' "

That throws Barbour for a second. Even *he* isn't in the business of calling a teacher a liar. "No, well, what I mean is, I don't think the rest of us knew whether the requirements were *hard* enough to earn a letter."

"So you basically made your decision without sufficient knowledge." It isn't a question.

"I think what Mike is trying to say," Benson says, "is

169

that we believed you were setting a standard for yourselves that would meet criteria that would set your team in an equal position with other sports teams."

Simet and Benson lock eyes. Simet says, "I haven't been a member of this council very long, but in almost every formal meeting I've attended elsewhere, the chairperson's job is to run the meeting and let the other members debate, to avoid an appearance of bias."

That pisses Benson off, and the jacked muscle in his jaw tells us so, but he's cool and hands the gavel to Roundtree. I don't think Benson knows *how* any formal meeting is run. He's used to saying what he wants when he wants. It doesn't matter which of them is chair, it still takes a vote away from the bad guys unless we're in a tie.

Carly says, "I wasn't here the day of the original vote, but it seems to me that if the council made a decision and the swimmers swam their entire season with that goal in mind, it would be unfair to change it now."

Go, Carly!

Barbour says, "We didn't know every kid on that team was gonna get a jacket."

"Neither did I," Simet says.

"But I think that may be the point," Benson says. "It's a brand-new sport here at Cutter, and every athlete lettered. What other sport in the school's history has lettered every athlete in the program?"

"Actually," Simet says, "the chess club lettered all its athletes in 1989 and again in '93." Now *how* in hell would Simet know that?

"The chess club!" Barbour blurts out. "That ain't no athletic team."

"It was then," Simet says. "Before '95 it was considered a

sports team, and the members earned letters. In those two years, every athlete lettered. No one said a word."

"Correction," Roundtree says. "Someone did say a word, which is why the chess club is no longer considered an athletic team. Chess is a game, not a sport."

"I won't get into that argument with you, Coach. Don't know whether I'd argue for or against chess as a sport. My point is, when it was considered one, everyone lettered. In context, there is precedent for all the athletes on a team lettering." The council is quiet, probably digesting Simet's words, but he raises his hands in mock surrender. "Hey, I don't even think it's a big deal, or has anything to do with the point of this issue. It's just a fact."

"Okay," Roundtree says. "Then let's focus on the issue. The item under discussion is whether the council had enough information when we took our last vote to make an intelligent judgment regarding the letter requirements of the swim team. Mr. Barbour thinks not, and it appears Coach Benson agrees. Is there more discussion, or should we vote to reconsider?"

My hand goes up. "Wait. How many other coaches had to bring their letter requirements before this council? I haven't been here before, but you guys didn't discuss basketball or volleyball or wrestling or any other winter sport, did you?"

Benson says, "The letter requirements for those sports have been set for a long time. Most often it's a question of rubber stamping, because the requirements are reasonable."

"So there are bylaws that say the council has the right to pass judgment on a coach or a team? Like, you could show me where all this is written down?"

Benson is really tightening up now. "It is understood at

171

this school, Mr. Jones, that the Athletic Council oversees all athletic matters. This unquestionably falls under our jurisdiction."

"But it's not written down," I say.

"It doesn't have to be written down."

"But it isn't."

"I've said all that needs to be said," Benson says, "and I'm asking that this be brought to a vote."

"Actually," Simet says, "I think it does have to be written down somewhere, Coach. I can't imagine that the purpose and criteria for this council isn't recorded somewhere. Is it possible to postpone this long enough to look into that? I won't order the letters yet, and we can hold off on making a decision until we see exactly how this is all laid out. That's fair, isn't it?"

Benson thinks it isn't and says so, but when put to a vote, waiting seems reasonable to a simple quorum. Thank God for women's sports and for Carly Hudson.

"I just wanted to regroup," Simet says back in his room. "That would have been too close to call. It will take them a while to dig up the paperwork, if there is any, and set up another meeting. We might have been able to pull the votes, but I didn't want to take a chance if we can do it without. If we can work up a little compassion for Chris and play down Mott's two-gun salute to the student body, we could have a shot."

Carly tells me afterward we should have gone ahead and called for a vote. She's afraid Janet Lindstrom might vote with Benson. It's a chance we'll have to take.

Workouts are a kick. We have put the supine surgical-tubing station (which Dan Hole began to call muscle masturbation—thereby placing him forever in Mott's good graces) into mothballs, and now the guys simply line up in an endless forty-by-infinite-yard relay, where they go after me forty yards at a time, and I build up incredible yardage. In the second week we'll taper me again, with medium-speed yards coupled with quality sprints, until I supposedly peak at some cardiomuscular apex that will allow me to lay waste to the swimmers on the coast, none of whom have I yet seen up close and personal.

To stay with me, each of my guys starts from a dive, which adds a little twist to my workout one out of four times when Simon hits the water hard enough to surf me into the next lane. When this is all over, I may try an open-water swim. I say one out of *four* times because Chris Coughlin works out on the other side of me, swimming as hard as he can, then waiting for me to lap him before coming after me again. He really does have some potential down the road, and Simet is keeping him in shape to see if he can get on an age-group team as soon as the state meet is over.

The music from the boom box is so loud Simet has to cup his hands and holler directly into my ear to correct the tiniest imperfections in my stroke, but it adds to the overall ambience and is not to be squelched. Somewhere near the end of the season, Jackie Craig became captivated by the music of John Philip Sousa, so now "Rudolph the Red-Nosed Reindeer" is sandwiched between "Stars and Stripes Forever" and "Semper Fidelis." Jackie didn't say a word; simply handed Simet the Sousa CDs when Simet called for new music as he did at the beginning of each week.

For the past two weeks we've been getting a lot of telephone hang-ups at home, which I assume is Rich Marshall slamming down the receiver every time he calls and Alicia doesn't answer. She does answer the phone as regularly as anyone else in the house, so sooner or later he'll get her.

"Gotta happen sometime," Dad told her. "Might as well see if you have the power to refuse him while you have some support." Mom thinks we should try to catch him and add a few extra weekends in the slammer for breaking the no-contact order, but Dad says we should simulate real life as much as possible, and there will be a time in the very near future when Alicia has to figure out whether or not she's going to be able to put the kids' best interests ahead of her own. Heidi is doing much better, which means she's meaner than a Doberman to her younger brothers, who have enjoyed Rich Marshall's umbrella protection plan from the day of their birth. A new pecking order is being established, and nothing in me wants to stop it.

The hang-ups prompt my mother to order Caller ID, and between that and Last-Call Callback we discover most of the calls are coming from the pay phone at the 7-Eleven about eight blocks away. One of Rich's logging truck drivers must have quit, so Rich is driving until he can hire another, and the convenience store is directly on his route.

Rich is also making his presence felt in more subtle ways. One day there is a Marshall Logging plastic travel coffee cup on the sidewalk across the street from the house. Another day a double-bitted ax is stuck in a tree in our backyard, a blue hard hat left in the vacant lot behind our place. We know it's him but have no proof. There are several hundred of the coffee cups strewn around town, remnants of a campaign ploy Rich used last year in a failed run for a city council position.

"He's watching us," Alicia says just after Dad pulls the ax from the tree trunk. "He's letting me know he's around."

174

Dad puts the ax in the garage, then stands in front of Alicia, placing his hands on her shoulders. "Tell me you haven't been communicating with him, Alicia."

"I haven't. Honest, Mr. Jones. Not once. Since I've been here, not once."

"I'm going to trust that," he says. "What do you think he'll do?"

She looks away, a flash of desperation passing over her face. "Something bad," she says. "Rich obeys the rules up to a point, then he doesn't care. When he thinks somebody is taking something that's his . . . See, he doesn't really care about the kids. I've always known that. It's when he thinks he's losing me." She nods toward me. "He thinks I'm . . . you know, because of Willis . . . When it gets bad, I don't know what would stop him."

Dad's face goes hard. "I'll stop him."

I'd put my money on Dad.

Late that night the phone rings, followed by an extra loud hang-up. Ten minutes later it rings again. Ten minutes later, again. All from 7-Eleven. Dad tells Alicia to answer it, then he and I hop in my car for a quick run to the store, where we discover Rich's pickup idling next to a row of three pay phones. We pull up on the far side of the building so we can watch him catty-cornered through the store windows. His pickup door opens, and he takes the few wobbly steps to the phone. It's obvious he doesn't know this state has an open-container law.

Like a cat, Dad is out of the car and at the door of the phone booth, his knee wedged against it to keep Rich trapped. He whacks the glass hard with his hand, and Rich turns with a start. "What the fuck?"

"Nobody's home," Dad yells through the door.

"Who the— Get the hell away from the door."

Dad opens it partway, blocking Rich from coming out. "Marshall, I'm standing here talking with you at midnight at a phone number that I can match up with my Caller ID, which means you've broken a no-contact order. It's hard to tell if you're dumber than you are mean, or the other way around, but I'm going to give you the benefit of the doubt and go with dumb. Which means if no one at my house hears from you for thirty days at least, I won't report this."

"Get the fuck away from me," Rich says. "Lemme outta here."

"Soon as you repeat back to me what I said," Dad says.

"GET THE FUCK AWAY FROM THE DOOR!" Rich screams, but Dad forces it closed.

"Repeat it," Dad says.

"Man, if you don't want your ass kicked—"

"I do want my ass kicked, Marshall. And I want you to be the one to try. Now, you're drunk and you're screwing up big time, and if I were you, I'd cut my losses and go home." Dad backs away from the door.

Rich comes out, looks like he's going after Dad, but he gets a better look and, even in his altered state, reconsiders, which to my way of thinking is a *very* smart move for a guy drunk on his ass.

Dad says, "Rich, I'm doing my best to be decent to you, but if you keep stalking, I could get pretty uncivil."

"Foster parent can't do that," Rich says. "You got rules."

"Yeah," Dad says. "I'm telling you, when it comes to protecting folks, I make my own rules."

"You got a lot of guts, messin' with a guy's family."

"And I wouldn't forget that," Dad says. "I've got a *lot* of guts."

Rich turns for his pickup. "For a baby killer," he says. "A lot of guts for a baby killer."

Dad shows no reaction.

"Better keep your hands off my wife, Sambo," Rich says as he brushes past me. "You and your daddy better watch your backs." He's in his truck and gone.

"You gonna call the cops?" I ask on the way back.

"We've got the evidence," Dad says. "I'll wait and see what happens with the calls and the artifacts. When a guy gets past a certain point, legal action just pisses him off. We don't want Rich thinking he has nothing to lose. That's the worst place for a stalker. If he thinks he can win something by staying away, maybe he will."

I repeat Rich's parting words.

"And we will watch our backs, won't we, son?"

I agree that we'll watch our backs.

Under normal circumstances Simet and I would take a school car or his Humvee to State, but he wants the team in on this and so arranges to borrow his uncle's Winnebago, a vehicle so wide it's illegal in three states. Luckily one of them isn't Washington.

Because I'm the only one swimming, and because our struggle with the Athletic Council has become public, the students lined up to see us off this time look like those being sent home for writing a threatening essay. No cheerleaders, no marching band, and—surprise!—no one from Wolverines Too, which was out en force when the football team boarded the bus for State.

The ride over is great. Icko manages the beast as if it is a super school bus, with Simet in the copilot's seat and the rest of us lounging in captain's chairs and sprawled out on the beds. Mott wants to get one of those transparent maps you put on your back window, skip the meet, and see how many states we can color in before anyone discovers we've told the school to kiss our ass.

"Better get a map of the world," Simon says. "It's a question of them *caring*."

Mott smiles from his sprawled-out position on the bed. "Better make it a map of the solar system." Which launches Dan Hole into some discourse on astrophysics, until Icko informs him he doesn't consider the season over yet, and Dan could "build up a real set of pecs talking about that stuff."

The meet is held at the University of Washington pool, a pretty impressive place if you've been swimming in backwater towns of eastern Washington and northern Idaho. The water is just as wet and the pool just as long, but there are seats for as many people as usually see a basketball game in Cutter. Teams from all over the state, male and female, dot the deck and fill the practice lanes, and hordes of fans yell encouragement from the bleachers.

My races are spread over two days. The hundred on the first, and the fifty and two hundred on the second. It's intimidating even though my times are fastest in the state for the hundred and the fifty. The other contenders are surrounded by teammates, all in flashy warm-ups with state-of-the-art workout bags, as opposed to my gray sweats and canvas bag.

The team officials won't let my guys onto the deck because they're not participating, so they stake out a spot low enough in the bleachers where I can hear them cheer, while Simet and I throw our stuff in a corner next to the starting blocks.

I swim the hundred tonight, the fifty and two hundred tomorrow. The instant I hit the water for warm-ups, I know the sprints belong to me. Simet and my Far Side swimming team have brought me to exactly the point I need to be: that place where my strength and stamina and timing meet at a perfect vortex. I *will* get off the blocks like a shot, and I *won't* miss a turn. And *no*body can take me in between. There are few times in your life when you *know*, but for me this is one of them. I swim some easy laps, some middle speed, a few pickups, and come out of the water confident.

Tay-Roy calls me over to the bleachers before my prelim to the hundred, leans over the rail. "You know, if you win just two events, Cutter will place ahead of a whole bunch of teams. You could put us in the top ten by yourself."

I do already know that. Simet has told me so many times there's no way I could forget. A good showing exonerates him from skipping out on the wrestling job.

"And if you won three—"

"I won't be winning the two hundred, Tay," I tell him. "I'll be lucky to place in the top six."

"Even that," he says.

Mott appears beside him. "Remember, this ain't just for you," he says. "If you're up in the team standings, *we're* up in the team standings. Don't want to put too much pressure on you. . . ." He laughs.

I blow my prelim field away, earning the fast lane for the finals. I'm nearly a full tenth of a second faster than the second-place time, and I do feel strong. I wish there were more drama, but I win the final by the same margin.

Before we head back to the Winnebago, Simet calls in my time to the TV stations in Spokane, so Cutter will get the news. He has fulfilled his promise, picked up valuable points for the All-Sport title. Another first would put us close to the top, and then even a fourth place could put us ahead going into spring sports. With the kind of track team we should have, we might wrap it up.

There isn't much more drama for the fifty than the hundred. I'm a couple of tenths off the state record after my prelim, and tie it in the final. Two firsts put us in eighth place in overall meet standings. The next relay knocks us out of the top ten because number nine and ten both have strong teams, so our ability to place in the top ten rests on whether or not I can hit my best two hundred.

I qualify fourth, first in my heat. Something is happening here that I recognize from times when it seemed like the universe was lining up athletically for me. My first hundred is within a half second of my best hundred time ever, and I finish easy, saving myself for the final. The two hundred has always been my toughest race, because when I'm supposed to turn it up on laps six and seven, I either don't turn it up far enough, or too far and then can't bring it home. But I'm in a zone, feeling stronger with each lap. If I can hold this till the final, I could surprise some folks.

We go back to the parking lot between the prelims and the finals to hang out and let a little pressure off. Simet uses his cell phone to leave Benson and Morgan messages, telling them I have exceeded his wildest dreams; that a good finish in the two hundred is a real possibility, and maybe they should start cleaning out a place in the trophy case for the All-Sport trophy. "Nothing wrong with greasing the skids," he tells us as he snaps the phone shut. "Be nice until we don't need them anymore."

We get the call back from Benson within five minutes.

Simet answers, listens, hands me the phone. "He was out shoveling the walk," Simet says.

I say, "Hey, Coach, what's up?"

"I hear you're knockin' 'em dead over there. We're all real proud of you."

I say thanks.

"Just the two hundred left?"

"Yes, sir."

"Can you win it?"

"Maybe if a kid named Ray Roscoe drowns in warm-ups. He's got Olympic trial times in the two and four hundred."

"Where's he from?"

"Wilson High. In Tacoma."

Benson is quiet a moment. Then, "They're no threat. Anyone there from Seattle Heights?"

"Two guys. Pretty good swimmers. I qualified a tenth of a second ahead of one and about a second behind the other."

"That's a problem."

"I was just swimming to qualify," I tell him. "I'm closer than that."

"They took us in a couple wrestling matches we should have won at their state meet yesterday. I've made the calculations, and I believe if you take them both, we'll go into spring in first place."

"Make you a deal."

He laughs. "Shoot."

"I beat both Seattle Heights swimmers, you vote for our letter requirements."

Silence. "I'll see what I can do."

"What you can do is raise your hand when the yes vote is called." I glance at Simet, who's shaking his head as if in warning.

Benson says, "T. J., you're not threatening to throw the two hundred, are you?"

"Did I ever tell you who my favorite baseball player of all time is?"

He doesn't answer.

"Shoeless Joe Jackson."

"Let me speak with your coach."

I hand the cell phone to Simet. Mott gives me thumbs up.

Chris Coughlin says, "They gots a baseball player with no shoes?"

"Shoeless Joe," I say. "Sometimes he didn't wear shoes."

"And sometimes," Dan Hole says, "he compromised his love of the game for his own personal, which is to say *financial*, gain."

"Yes, he did," I say.

Icko glances at Dan as if to say, "The season isn't over yet, my pearly-mouthed friend," and Dan smiles.

Simet listens into the cell phone, glances at me, then at the rest of the team. "Coach, that'll never hold up. You waited until we were gone." Pause. "Maybe that's true, but there was no hurry." He listens another moment, then says, "I'll think about it, Coach, but I can't promise." Then, "Okay, I *won't* promise."

He waits, holds the phone away from his ear, grimacing at Benson's tirade.

"Coach, that may or may not be a good coaching technique, but it doesn't work with *peers*, okay?" Pause. "Well, maybe not in your eyes, but technically I am your peer. Listen, why don't you let us take care of business here and you have your weekend. There have to be some good games on." Pause. "Yeah, sure, we'll keep you informed."

He flips the phone shut, gazes into our faces. "Coach

182

Benson told me not to tell you this until after the meet; I said I'd think about it." He puts a finger to his temple and glances toward the heavens. "There. I've thought about it. They held an Athletic Council meeting Friday."

"Lemme guess," Tay Roy says. "They voted on our letter requirements."

Simet's eyebrows arch. "That's cowardly," he says. "I was gone, and Janet Lindstrom voted with Benson and Roundtree." He slams his fist into his hands. "I could have talked them into it. *Damn* it! Don't worry, guys, this isn't over."

I am pissed. This is exactly the reason I've never turned out for anything; they always have to have it their way. They seem to listen, but in the end they make the rules and to hell with the people who have to follow them. They have no respect for what we did, no respect for what we created out of thin air.

We're deflated. We are eight laps from the end of our season and have met every goal we set.

"This isn't over, guys," Coach says again. "They can't *set* the letter requirements, they only have right of refusal. I'll get us what I can."

That doesn't wipe the look of dejection off most of my teammates' faces. Mott isn't dejected at all. He's pissed. I'm with him.

"I don't know whether this helps," Simet says, "but there's one thing they can never take from us, and that's this time. As a young man I coached swimmers on their way to the Olympic trials. I've coached championship teams at all levels, but I have never coached a team with the guts this team has. When I'm looking back on my coaching career, this is the team I'll be proudest of."

He means it—we know it, feel it—and it still feels like

hell. For everyone here but me, and possibly Tay-Roy, this is the way it always is. Do your best and get the crumbs.

I grab my tank suit, and we start for the door, when the sounds of sobbing turn us around. Jackie Craig sits in the captain's chair behind the driver's seat, his body convulsing.

Chris Coughlin watches him with anxiety you can almost feel. Icko walks over and puts a hand on Jackie's forearm. Mott says, "Hey, man, them fuckin' jackets are ugly anyway."

Jackie gasps for air, convulses again, shaking his head.

"Naw, really," Mott says, "they are."

"It's not the jackets," Jackie says, doubling his word count for the season. "It's . . ."

We wait while he works to catch his breath.

"It's . . . I don't know what I'm going to do when this is over. I never belonged to . . . *anything*. I was never on a team, never chosen for . . ." He stops, breathes again. "When I got on this team, I couldn't believe it. I kept wondering when you guys were going to find me out and make me leave. The reason I haven't said anything all year was so you wouldn't notice me. I didn't want to *bump* anything, you know? It's like when there's a mean dog, you just stand there and hope he doesn't see." He closes his eyes and shakes his head from side to side. "What happens when this is over? God, what am I gonna do?"

Icko grips Jackie's shoulder. "You're gonna do whatever you have to do to keep this alive," he says. "We ain't a mean dog. Right now, you're gonna get up and help T. J. swim this race. Then we're gonna order some hella pizza, as you guys say, an' have us a goddamn victory party."

"Hell," Mott says, "none of us could swim worth a shit. We'll find somethin' else we can't do worth a shit an' turn

184

out for that in the spring. Wanna coach a rugby team, sir? Then, hell, come summer, maybe we'll turn out for Little League."

Because I qualified fourth in the two hundred, I don't have an inside lane, but I kept myself out of fifth and sixth spots, so I'll still be close enough to see the leaders.

Warm-up feels good, my stroke powerful. This is it. I'm planning the race as I swim, accelerating into my turns and coming out of them as if on a sling.

Ray Roscoe warms up two lanes over, and we're gliding through the water stroke for stroke. For a brief second I wonder—if everything goes just right, could I take him?

The guys line up low on the bleachers, waving their towels in support. Apart from Tay-Roy, they look wounded, once again handed second-class citizenship. I hate Benson; I hate Barbour. Those assholes set us up—man, they have to have it all—and all of a sudden I have new resolve for this race.

The starter calls us to the blocks—"Swimmers, take your marks." The starting gun pops and I am stretched out over the water, surging with the adrenaline my fury creates.

14

The ride home is a trip. We stay long enough to collect my hardware and say good-bye to some of the other swimmers, then load up the Winnebago, stop in Issaquah long enough to take on a cargo of pizza and soft drinks, and get out on I-90 for the four-hour trip home. In the foothills of the Cascades rain begins, turning to snow as we climb toward Snoqualmie Pass.

Simet tells Icko to please not wreck the Winnebago, since we are laid out in it like our first college apartment, and it would be hard to explain to the state police why no one was strapped in.

"Won't have to explain it," Icko says. "We'll all be dead."

Dan explains to Chris that no one is really going to die, and though Chris doesn't understand one word in five, he has learned to mine Dan's tone for the meaning to his sentences. Chris Coughlin is no dummy.

It's quiet at first, and I believe I'm not the only one thinking about Jackie's words. He said what the others were afraid to say, that the worst thing about being a loner is getting the chance not to be, then having to go back. I don't want to talk about endings; this whole thing feels too good to do it only once. I say, "Coach, what are we gonna do about the letter jackets?"

Simet says, "We're gonna wear 'em with pride."

"We know *how*," Mott says. "What we wanna know is *if*."

Simet turns his captain's chair around to face us. "Those guys made an agreement," he says. "They can't wait until we're gone, and then go back on it. I'll take this right out of school and into court."

Whoa.

Jackie stares out the window. For him the jackets mean nothing. It's being here. I lean over and put my hand in the middle of his back. "Don't worry, buddy. We got good times ahead. You ever play any roundball?"

"At home in my driveway," he says. And then, quietly, "By myself."

"Well, start working on your jumper and get ready for evolution. We're gonna rise out of the water to the hard court. Hoopfest, here we come."

"T. J., I've seen you play. You don't want me on your Hoopfest team."

"I've already won Hoopfest. I mean, look at these assholes," I say, waving my hand grandly over the premises. "We looked pretty different in swimming gear; imagine us in basketball stuff."

Jackie probably doesn't believe me, but I'm dead serious. I see us as a team of role players, very different from other three-on-three teams I've put together. There's a challenge here. I look at Mott, can't decide whether I like the idea of a one-legged psycho swimmer better than a one-legged psycho hoopster. But that's for early summer. If we can't turn them around on the letter jacket thing, I say we go with Mott's idea of rugby for the spring. Or maybe Australian-rules football.

* * *

187

I walk into the Athletic Council meeting ready for the worst. Simet has shamed them into calling an emergency meeting by accusing Cutter High's male coaching fraternity of cowardice—that's the word he used—for the recall on our letters while we were out of town, "attending the State meet, for Christ's sake." Now they're not only pissed off at me, they're pissed off at my coach.

Barbour asks what I'm doing there. "He's not a member of this council," he says. "This is the *Athletic* Council."

Benson tells Barbour to cool it but agrees. "T. J., you don't have any business here."

Simet says, "He's here as my guest." It must not seem worth the fight to Benson, who lets it ride.

We sit at the long, rectangular wooden table in uneasy silence, and Benson calls the meeting to order. Since it's an emergency meeting called for a specific purpose, he tells us, there is no reason for formalities. "Let's get to the business at hand, which is the council's taking another look at the letter requirements for the swimming team. As you know, Coach Simet and T. J., we took a vote last week and agreed that there needs to be a reassessment."

Simet says, "I am aware of that, and I believe there is some question as to whether that was a 'legal' vote."

"It was decided on by a quorum," Roundtree says. "That's the democratic process."

"The democratic process," Simet says, "doesn't include waiting until the opposition is out of town to make decisions. I'm going to make this short. I've reviewed the original charter for this council, which goes back to 1955. There is not one piece of paperwork that gives this council the power to dictate the letter requirements for any sport. It has been true, *without exception*, that the coach of the

188

sport sets the letter requirements for that sport. I will challenge your power to do it differently in a court of law if I have to."

There are protests and veiled threats, all of which go past Simet as if he isn't in the room. The council decides to discuss it with Morgan, and possibly the school board, before making a decision.

"You have no decision to make," Simet says. "This is entirely out of your realm of control. You should know I've consulted an attorney."

"Who said what?" Benson asks.

"Who said, 'Bring it.' "

These guys are *pissed*, but for the moment Simet seems to hold the cards. Barbour looks at me as if he'd like to come over the table and take me out right there, and I couldn't wish for anything more.

"Very well," Benson says. "We'll take that under advisement, maybe talk with the district's counsel. I have one more thing I'd like an answer to."

Simet says, "Shoot."

"This is for Jones."

I lean forward on my elbows on the tabletop, feeding off Simet's strength.

Benson says, "Jones, tell us about the two hundred freestyle at State."

"Not much to tell," I say. "I never felt better."

"And you finished sixth?"

"Dead last," I say.

When the gun sounded for the two hundred at State, it was like I said—I never felt stronger. But back at Cutter, all they wanted were the points. They didn't care how Jackie Craig or Andy Mott or Simon DeLong or Dan Hole or Chris Coughlin walked away feeling. They just wanted the points.

Words can't do justice to the sensation of the cool water rushing over my shoulders and back, my stroke nearly perfect through the entire race. I finished the second hundred faster than the first, and a full thirty seconds slower than my fastest time. And we go into spring six points behind in our quest for the All-Sport trophy.

"I think you tanked that race, Jones. I looked at your time."

"I prefer to think I just ended my season a couple of minutes early," I say.

"You have no respect for anything."

"Sure I do, Coach. I have respect for the guys I swam with and the season we made. What I don't have any respect for is you guys."

Benson looks out the window, gathers himself, then calls an end to the meeting.

"Wait," Barbour says. "You mean that's it? We don't have anything to say about this? These guys wear Cutter blue and gold? Man, *I* could swim faster than at least four of those guys."

Before I even think, I say, "Tell you what, Barbour. If you can stay with Chris Coughlin for one workout, we'll end this discussion for good. No letters, no litigation, no whining. But same for you. If you can't, you shut the hell up."

"Chris *Coughlin*?" he says. "That little reta—punk?"

"Yeah," I say. "That little retard. Three-thirty Monday afternoon. He'll be waiting."

"That okay with you, Mr. Simet?" Barbour says.

Simet plays it just right, shaking his head. "I don't know. Chris . . ."

Barbour goes on the offensive. "Come on, you heard the offer," he says. "It's coming from the captain of the team."

Simet glances at me as if he wants to wash my mouth out with soap, takes a deep breath. "You want to take that back, T. J.?"

I hesitate.

"What's the matter, tough guy?" Barbour says. "Open your mouth a little too quick?"

"The offer stands."

Barbour says, "I'll be there."

Simet looks to the rest of the council. "How about it, folks? At least we could end in agreement."

There is talk of this being highly irregular, but in fairly short order agreement is reached. If Chris Coughlin can outlast Mike Barbour in the water, the members of the swim team get their letters.

Back in Simet's office, I congratulate him on his abilities as a thespian. This is a better deal than the original. Chris Coughlin has been in the water every day for three months. He was a pretty good little swimmer before he started; it was Chris who gave me the idea for all this in the first place. I don't care what kind of athlete Barbour is, he won't last. If you're going to be a swimmer, you gotta swim.

While we were at State, Rich Marshall turned up the heat, calling the house from pay phones all over town and slamming down the phone when he heard a voice that wasn't Alicia's. Alicia agreed not to answer under any circumstances, and she was holding to her word, though she said the rings themselves were starting to sound threatening, as if he were able to turn the bell inside the phone malicious.

So this afternoon Mom is at work and Dad is in the garage working on some bikes, she picks it up on the first ring, and lo and behold, guess who. He says if she'll meet him with the kids just once more, he'll leave her alone for good. He's in his contrite mode, begging that a man should be allowed to see his sons. They argue about whether she'll bring Heidi, but in the end she has to, or Heidi will tell my parents they're gone. She hollers to Dad out in the garage that she's going to take the kids up into the trees in the large vacant lot behind the house to make a snowman, and loads them up.

By the time Dad figures out they're not in the vacant lot, there's no way to track them down, so he calls the cops and waits. It's after dinner when they come home. Alicia lies and says she decided to take the kids to buy some toys at a little secondhand toy store about three miles from the house. When Mom asks her to produce the toys, she can't, and Thing Two says, "We saw Daddy!" Heidi sits in the wooden rocker over by the fireplace, thumb crammed into her mouth to the hilt, staring at the fire.

Dad tells Alicia she'd better pack her stuff, because when he reports to her caseworker in the morning, she'll surely have to move out, and Alicia goes into meltdown, sobbing and begging for another chance. Thing One and Thing Two gather around her and kind of pet her head; Heidi never gets out of the chair.

And then the phone rings.

Dad picks it up to the click of the handset being slammed down. When Rich started calling over the weekend, Dad researched the locations of the phone booths through the phone company as the numbers popped up on Caller ID. Tonight he puts a piece of paper by the phone and traces Rich's movements. By the tenth or eleventh call, a pattern appears.

Dad gets the videocamera out of the closet and picks up his cell phone. "Plug a phone and a Caller ID gadget into the computer line," he tells me. "When you see my cell phone number, pick up. It should come right on the heels of a pay phone call on the other line."

My mom asks what he's doing.

"I'm gonna get him on this no-contact order," he says. "It's not valid for Alicia now, because she was the one who broke it, but it's good for us. The camera records the time of the shot, and Caller ID does the same. I'll zoom in on him and take it to the cops. Let him cool his heels in the slammer for a few more weekends."

Mom says, "John Paul, why don't you just call the police and let them do this?"

"Because they don't do it. It's low priority until after he hurts someone, and truthfully, Rich Marshall has too many friends on the force. He's been getting away with crap for years." He moves toward the door with determination. "We should have hit him with everything we had back when he shot the deer out from under T. J."

Mom tells him to be careful as Heidi comes through the kitchen door, one hand dripping soapsuds, the other dripping blood. Mom rushes to her. "Heidi, what *happened*?"

"It works!" Heidi says, touching her raw forearm.

Mom takes a Brillo pad from her other hand.

I close my eyes. "She found something to take the brown off. God*damn* it!"

"Who told you to do this?" Dad says.

Heidi doesn't look up, runs her fingers over her forearm. "Daddy Rich."

Dad's out the door.

Mom and Alicia take Heidi to clean up her arm, while

193

Mom tells Alicia this is *her* doing. I haven't seen my mother this pissed since I peed on the hot steam radiator when I was five.

As if the minor gods in charge of jerks are doing their job, the telephone starts ringing from phone booths at about ten-minute intervals, which means Rich has gone into dumb-shit mode, driving directly from one to the next. I call Dad on the cell phone and we follow him. "Just look for that stupid red dualie," I tell him. "Very photogenic automobile."

He says, "How's Heidi?"

"Georgia's on her way over. She's okay, I think. I mean, shit, it's hard to tell. Mom and Alicia are fixing her arm."

The line goes dead.

There is a certain way my dad gets that makes you nervous; kind of the opposite of his Zen, let-it-be self, and this cold, get-the-job done countenance is a good indicator.

The main-line phone rings three more times without a follow-up call from Dad, then on the fourth they ring almost simultaneously. "Hey," I say.

"Is the phone ringing?"

"Yup."

"Got him," Dad says. "I'll get him on tape a couple more times. Be sure the Caller ID registers time and date."

I check it. "It is. Dad?"

"What?"

"Then what?"

"Then I'm going to have a little talk with Rich Marshall about how to treat kids."

"Where are you?"

"Never mind, T. J. He's already got the racial thing going with you. I don't want you anywhere near this."

194

"Okay," I say. "But tell me where you are anyway, just in case something happens, and I need to call the cops."

Dad knows me too well. "I've got my cell phone right here. If I need cops, I'll call cops."

Shit.

"You wait there and make sure the technology is working."

We have Call Waiting on both lines, so I can use the phone while I'm waiting for Dad to call again, and I do that to call AT&T to track down the pay phone locations, but those guys are nine-to-fivers and I would have to "push 1, 2, or 3" a whole bunch of times just to find out they will be with me tomorrow.

The next call comes from Rich, followed quickly by Dad.

"He's calling," I say. "Turn on that camera and make him famous."

"No sooner said than done," Dad says. "One more for safety's sake." And the line goes dead.

But my daddy's not so smart as him thinks, as Chris Coughlin might say, because I recognize the next number that comes up from having given it to Carly's dad about ten times one night when I wanted her to call me back at Wolfy's. I don't know what'll go down when Dad and Rich Marshall come face-to-face, but if it's at Wolfy's, Dad could easily be outnumbered by a whole lot of folks with Rich's sensibilities, so I'm moving down the road in my speedy Corvair in the time it takes me to tell Mom to watch the phones. She wants to call the cops, but I convince her not to crank this up bigger than it needs to be as I'm walking out the door. The look in my father's eyes when he saw Heidi's arm keeps my foot heavy on the pedal.

Wolfy's is less than a mile from the house, and Dad is

putting the camera away as I pull into the lot, gets almost to the door before he sees me.

"Goddamn it, T. J., I told you to stay there."

I look through the front window at Rich talking to Mike Barbour and a couple of his friends. I tell him I'm just here for crowd control.

He walks in and right up to Rich, shoving his fingers deep on either side of his Adam's apple, pushing the back of his head against the window. It's so quick and silent most of the patrons don't even turn to look. Marshall gasps for air. In my dad's softest voice he says, "Marshall, I've got you on tape three times calling our house, which is a direct breach of the no-contact order. I'm not sure how many times you have to hear this to believe it, and I can barely believe I'm giving you one more chance. About forty-five seconds before I left the house, your stepdaughter came out of the bathroom with her forearm bleeding because she tried to change the color of her skin with a Brillo pad. *You* told her it would work."

Barbour moves toward Dad and so do I, shaking my head. "You should be home resting for your swim competition."

"Fuck you, Jones."

We glare, but he stays put, and Dad finishes his proposition. "Now, I can run these pictures over to the police and let you have a few days more in the slammer, or you and I can make an agreement right here and now that you have called my house, and stalked your family, for the last time."

"This is assault," Rich squeaks through a partially closed windpipe.

"Yes, it is," Dad says.

"Fuck you," Rich says. He sounds like Donald Duck, and Dad pinches harder.

196

"That's not the right answer."

Rich's face is bright red, headed through the rainbow toward darker colors. He can't talk, so he nods his head in panic, and Dad loosens his grip. By now patrons are noticing something is wrong, and the night manager starts around the counter. "Is there a problem here?"

Dad looks at Rich. "Is there a problem here, Rich?"

Rich's mouth is pinched, moving toward a sneer, but he says, "No. No problem."

"Good," Dad says, and looks at the manager. "No problem, Sam. I'm sorry if I stirred things up. We'll be going," and he moves toward the door.

I back out behind him because I don't trust either Marshall or Barbour any further than I could punt them. Rich stands massaging his throat and glaring at Dad, and then me, with pure hatred.

15

The next morning what little slack there is between Barbour and me is drawn tighter than a bowstring. He stands around with his blockers watching my every move, as if somehow that will intimidate me. What he doesn't know is I'm visualizing his muscular body sinking to the bottom of the pool at All Night when skinny little Chris Coughlin swims him into submission. He has no idea how badly I want a clean shot at him myself, a little self-defense action to render him infirm. Under normal circumstances I could bait him in front of his friends and bring him right at me, but Dad was clear that he doesn't want any escalation with Marshall *or* Barbour. The connection between Rich and Mike is unclear, but it's definitely there, and the bottom line is that Heidi and the twins have to be kept safe at all costs and, of course, if we can pull Alicia back under the umbrella, hooray for us.

Georgia was there when we got back last night, working through Heidi's stuff with her, and before she left, she stopped in my room.

"Don't want you getting into a bunch of mess over this," she said. "You got to be a professional. You work for me."

"But as a professional," I said back, "you've got no problem with my defending myself."

"No, but I have a problem with you creating a situation where you have to defend yourself." Georgia knows me like a well-read book. She said, "You listen to me, and I told your daddy the same thing. The way Rich Marshall is acting right now tells us he's less rational than usual, which means he's not rational at *all*. And it wouldn't be all that hard to get that Barbour boy cranked up right with him. They may not be brothers, but they came out from under the same rock, which means if you mess with one of 'em, you're messing with the other. If you want to kick somebody's ass, you get some gloves and do it in the ring."

I told her I had an even better plan than that. I had somebody lined up to do the ass kicking for me.

The scenario at All Night Fitness is almost surreal. Several coaches and a couple of athletes from the Athletic Council are there, along with football players to cheer Barbour on. Icko runs the workout to avoid the appearance of a conflict of interest, while Benson and Simet watch from the pool deck. Simet was quick to agree to that; he knows the story about Icko bending rebar for Barbour's benefit back when Barbour was still threatening Chris about wearing his brother's jacket.

Chris is big-time pissed at me. "Why I gots to do it?" he says. "Why not somebody with muscles like Tay-Roy?"

" 'Cause you're the guy who can take him," I say, "and because you've got a reason to get even. Remember how he scared you?"

"He scares me right this minute," Chris says. "What if I beat him, and then he finds me alone by myself?"

Mott is behind us, listening. He leans forward and whispers into Chris's ear. "If he finds you alone, I'll beat him to death with my steel leg. And that's a promise. And I'll go over and tell him that right now if you want me to."

"Like just take it off and whack him?" Chris says.

"Right across the side of his ugly head," Mott says back.

That's a good visual for Chris, but he's still worried. The rest of the team gathers around him while Barbour steps out of his sweats. He's pretty impressive physically, and that brings back Chris's demons. I tell Tay-Roy to take off his shirt, which he does just to let Chris make the comparison.

"Okay," I say. "So we got more muscles on our side, and a steel leg. All you have to do is get in the water and keep swimming until that scumbag quits. You don't even have to swim faster than he does, just longer. Okay?"

Jackie steps forward and ruffles Chris's hair. He says, "Kick his ass," and Chris breaks into a big grin. Nobody has ever heard Jackie Craig say ass. Then Dan puts a hand on Chris's shoulder. "It's only about tenacity, Christopher. Tenacity will get the task completed here."

Chris watches Barbour, stretching and hyperventilating, across the pool. Though his buddies are kidding and cheering him on, Barbour shows no signs of humor. And he isn't looking over here at Chris. He's looking at me.

I'm looking back.

Icko tells them both to get in and warm up. Chris takes a hundred yards at about three-quarter speed, ten or twelve deep breaths between, and repeats, warming up like he has every day for the past four months. He looks good in the water, comfortable. I'm proud of him.

Barbour takes a couple of laps and says he's ready. Simet stands next to Benson with a big smile. This won't take long.

Icko brings them up to the blocks. "You said you can take Chris in the short stuff, right, Mike?"

"Whaddaya mean?"

"I heard you say you could take him for a hundred yards. Do you still think that?"

"Hell, yes. What does it matter? This isn't a race."

"I know," Icko says, "but we do interval training, and to keep it fair I want to be sure the intervals are equal. If you're about the same speed, you get the same intervals between. So we're doing ten one-hundred-yard swims, leaving the blocks every two minutes. The faster you swim, the more rest you get."

Barbour says, "Let's just do it."

This poor bastard has no idea what he's in for.

Icko starts them, and Barbour flies out over the water with a grunt. He swims ahead of Chris, but Chris catches him coming off the wall, having learned to flip at the deep end. Barbour touches him out, but he comes up gasping, where Chris is barely breathing hard.

Mott quickly organizes a lottery, and we each throw in a buck. We have Barbour dying anywhere from two hundred to seven hundred yards. I pick five.

He's dust in four, actually has to be helped out of the water. It's all we can do to get Chris to stop. He's into this swimming thing.

I can't help myself. I walk over to the other footballers and offer to let them make it a relay. Barbour has regained enough breath to say, "Fuck you, Jones. In case it slipped your mind, one swimmer didn't hit his best time every time. You tanked that last race. You're the only guy who doesn't letter."

"I know, Barbour. Some things just couldn't get any better."

Jackie gets Chris out of the water and jumps around the deck with him. On his own, Chris walks over to Barbour and sticks out his hand. He says, "You beat me on the first one. That was pretty good."

"Get away from me, you little retard!"

Chris is stricken; he has no defense for that.

I start back toward Barbour, but Simet yells my name. "It just tells you how bad he got beat."

Barbour tells him to go to hell.

Benson tells Barbour to get hold of himself, and Simet pats Benson on the back and says he might want to run his boys through a Dale Carnegie course in the off season.

Mott and Dan pat Chris on the back and tell him he just won us all letter jackets, and Simon puts him on his shoulders.

Barbour is long gone, but Benson comes over to tell Chris he did a hell of a job. And he apologizes for Barbour calling him a name.

"You should get him in trouble," Chris says. "He don't sposed to call me that."

It's hard to say much about the rest of the year. We sit at our own table for the winter sports banquet, and when time comes to introduce us and talk of our accomplishments, Simet makes them sound like those of any sport, never mentioning when he talks about "third-place points" that there were only three swimmers in the water, or that sometimes they were ready to turn out the lights by the time we finished.

We voted Chris "Most Inspirational," and if there is anything that will be indelibly burned into my consciousness about this season, it's the look on Chris's face when Coach hands him the trophy. He giggles until I think he'll pee his pants, then he touches the gold-plated swimmer at the top, which is pretty muscular, and says, "It gots Tay-Roy up here."

Tay-Roy winks at him and makes a muscle.

Then Simet hands out our letters, never mentioning the controversy but letting the parents of the other athletes know what an amazing group of guys this is. "Today the quality of the Cutter athlete is elevated," he says. "We began the year with only one true swimmer on the team. Most of these guys turned out with no idea what they were in for. The pool was too short, and the lanes weren't wide enough. We worked out a system for dry-land swimming so we could keep everyone working all the time. Some days the air and water in the pool were so warm I thought guys would pass out, but not one did, and not one ever backed off."

He rubs the back of his neck. "This was a different kind of team than I've coached. Jackie Craig said his first words on the way to the State meet. He just showed up twice every day and swam his heart out. Dan Hole turned us Shakespearean, and Tay-Roy kept us supplied with interested females." Coach smiles wider and shakes his head. "And Simon DeLong." Simon waves to the crowd. "You may have noticed that Simon does not have the body design of the swimmers you see atop the Olympic starting blocks, but let me tell you, folks, this kid has a sweet breaststroke and backstroke, and if he stays with it, in another year you won't recognize him." Then he says, "I don't know an athlete in the world with more courage than Andy Mott," and he doesn't elaborate.

"Every one of these guys, every time he swam, with one exception, hit his best time, which was the criteria we set for our letters, which I will now present."

We don't get the jackets yet—that happens at an all-school ceremony at the end of the year—but Coach calls each swimmer up to accept the certificate. Everyone but me.

* * *

The afternoon my guys actually get the jackets, a few days after the state track meet and a week and a half before graduation, might just be the highlight of my high school career. Morgan calls the new lettermen down to the gym floor team by team, makes a *long* speech about the tradition of Wolverine athletics, how everyone who wears the blue and gold is a cut above, an elite athlete in an elite program. "We are the envy of our conference," he says.

All the first-year lettermen stand in front—flanked by the second- and third-year lettermen—each receiving a jacket in a blue box tied in gold ribbon. When they announce the swim team, Carly and I stand and cheer, and they all throw a fist into the air. That plays to mixed reviews in the bleachers until Mott pulls up his pants leg, unhooks his leg, and thrusts it high into the air. The gym goes *quiet.* This is way better than his middle finger, because how can you suspend a guy for holding up his leg? He hands it to Jackie, who is taken off guard a moment, then thrusts it high. Andy Mott swam this entire swimming season on one leg, and not one kid outside the team even knew it.

And in the end I live up to my name. The Tao—the *real* Tao, that knows and *is* everything—celebrates irony. Nothing exists without its opposite. I didn't earn a letter jacket because I could, and all my friends did because they couldn't. Some things really don't get any better.

And some things do. Chris taps Simet on the shoulder, and Simet calls me down to the gym floor. I work my way down through the crowd, watching Chris retrieve a paper sack he has hidden behind him. When I reach him, he pulls out a blue-and-gold jacket and hands it to me.

"I don't get a jacket, Chris. I slowed up at State, remember?"

Simet says, "Take a closer look."

I unfold the jacket, and my throat closes over. Across the back it says, COUGHLIN, on the front it says, BRIAN.

"My brother would of been glad if I gave you this," Chris says. "So I did."

It would be nice to say the year ends on this note, that we walk away feeling bigger and better because we set a goal and met it, that a bunch of obscure guys who never had friends before, now have friends and life looks different. And that's all true, but that isn't how it ends.

I talk the guys into switching sports through spring, into getting ready for Hoopfest. If you think we didn't look like swimmers, you should see how much less we look like basketball players. After our third practice Mott says, "Let's do this like the Chicago Bulls did when they had Michael Jordan. You find some guys who can play this worthless sport, and we'll be your entourage." The other guys are quick to agree.

My dad is a pretty fair ballplayer, particularly under the boards, and Simet is one of those rare animals like me, a good athlete on land or sea. We need a fourth, and I pen in Mott's name, because though he doesn't move real well on the court, he can put down three pointers with alarming regularity. After a few practices we discover he can also place the alley-oop pass pretty well, which could come in handy when we want to surprise a team for those last two or three points. We enter ourselves in the open division, knowing that will pit us against some tough teams, but we'll be competitive.

We call ourselves the Slam-Dunking Mermen, in deference to our entourage, who attend most of our practices over at All Night and give us regular scouting reports on the Bushwhackers, Rich Marshall and Mike Barbour's team. With any luck, fate will not stack us up against them, but they are in the same division, so it's not unthinkable. If both teams keep winning (or losing, for that matter), we could run into them. Part of me would like to see that happen, and part of me wants to avoid it like STDs.

Barbour hates our entire team worse than ever, because somewhere a little after Easter break Kristen Sweetwater finally called it quits with him and was able to stay with it. It probably helped that Tay-Roy started putting moves on her on the heels of Barbour humiliating her yet again, and Tay-Roy has far less tolerance for her acceptance of that kind of behavior. He told her no girl he was with would *ever* be subjected to it, and if she started to go back with Barbour, he'd kick Barbour's ass. It would be a true battle of the Titans, and I don't know who'd walk away the victor, but I've watched Tay-Roy's resolve as a swimmer and as a bodybuilder, and if you're going to take him on, you'd better bring a lunch. Tay-Roy is old school. If something doesn't look right and it falls within his sphere of influence, he influences it.

The Slam-Dunking Mermen look a little different than the run-of-the-mill four-man teams early on a Saturday morning in late June on the first day of Hoopfest. Of ten thousand players, filling up three full blocks of downtown Spokane, we are the only team with a uniformed entourage. They wear the same T-shirts we wear, with a picture of a carp horizontal to the basket, stuffing the ball. Dan Hole is never three feet away from his clipboard, on which he records our stats with the consistency and accuracy of a computer. Chris Coughlin cheers loudly in his letter jacket, though the temperature will probably top out at eighty-five degrees, and Tay-Roy, whose chest expands the T-shirt so much the carp looks like an eel, holds Kristen's hand. Simon, whose T-shirt expands the other way so the carp looks like a whale, and Jackie Craig, who wears swim fins, man the Gatorade cooler. Carly is playing on a team of her own, so most of the time we're playing simultaneously. When we're not, we find her and bring to bear the full power of our outlandish support. She and her teammates like it better when we're playing simultaneously. My mother does not come downtown for this. She says she'll just bring our medical cards to the hospital.

The range of talent in the open division is wide. Most contestants have experience in organized ball, and the majority at least played on a varsity team in high school. A few have played in college. We draw a team that's way out of its league for our first game, so Simet and I rotate out and let Dad and Mott do most of the scoring, Dad from underneath and Mott from beyond the three-point line. Mott's in shorts today, his bionic leg exposed to the general public for the first time. He really is deadly from long range. Every time he sinks one, Chris goes out of his mind. During time-outs Mott walks over and rubs Chris's head for luck. Jackie has gotten down the art of clapping the swim fins, which adds a decidedly strange sound to our successes.

They come toward us like a twister in the distance, the black funnel cloud adjusting its trajectory no matter how you try to dodge it. Each time we finish a game and check the postings, which go up almost immediately on the side of a truck trailer parked at Hoopfest Central, we see the Bushwhackers headed right at us. If we each win our last games today—Saturday—we meet at 8:00 Sunday morning.

I imagine they would love that. All bragging aside, I'm the best player on either team, but Marshall has Dad over-matched, and Barbour and Simet are too close to call. Their point guard, Alex Neilson, plays at Spokane Community College, and their fourth man is Thurman Weeks, the sixth man on our high school team. Man for man they outmatch us, and if this were four-on-four, we'd be dust. But one guy is on the sidelines at all times, so we have a fair chance.

Our final game on Saturday is close, but we play tough and win it by four. Barbour and Marshall annihilate the team they play, and we're set for morning.

Dad invites everyone over for dinner in the evening and to set up our strategy for the game. Icko, who has been working most of the day and missed our heroics, supplies juicy burgers from Burger King and a whole bunch of soft ice cream. He tells us the burgers were left over, but they're hot and tender and I'm pretty sure he used part of his day's wages to feed us. Of all the guys likely to lose something when this team breaks up, he stands to lose as much as any. He was living by himself at All Night when I met him, staying out of sight and trying to put his son through college. Now he's adopted us. I swear the guy would do anything for any one of us.

Sunday breaks cool and clear. By 7:30 players stream toward the courts like lemmings. The air is filled with the sound of bouncing balls, balls careening off front rims and backboards, interspersed with the sweet swish of a thousand shots touching nothing but the bottom of the net. The Bushwhackers are on the court when we arrive. Rich sneers at me and watches my dad as if he were the true enemy in a real war.

Except for Chris Coughlin, we ignore them. Chris paces

the sidelines, watching Barbour and Marshall as if they were man-eating tigers, his letter jacket snapped to the top as if he thinks one of them is going to strip it off.

Tay-Roy stands on the sidelines beside Kristen, ignoring Barbour's existence.

The game has every possibility of turning sour from the beginning. Heidi came down to watch us all day yesterday and is now a fan of Spike Lee proportions. When it was clear we would play the Bushwhackers this morning, it was agreed that she and Alicia would stay home, but Heidi was inconsolable, particularly after Dad had said he's going to be shooting from the bleachers to keep from getting beat up underneath all day. Heidi is literal. We tell her Daddy Rich will be there and that he'll be playing against us, and she wants to go anyway. We call Georgia, and she says if Alicia is willing to show Heidi that she can protect her from Rich, it might even be good for the kid. Georgia thinks she'd like to take in a day of Hoopfest herself and will come down to walk Heidi and Alicia through it if need be.

It is a mistake.

They get first outs. I'm on Barbour, Dad's got Rich, and Simet is on Alex Neilson. Mott and Weeks will sub. We play better than we have a right to play, probably because Rich has seen the twins and Heidi with Alicia and Georgia, and it gets into his head. He calls Dad Pops and works him over inside, but Dad is patient and pulls down several offensive boards and gets a couple of put-backs. For most games there is only a court monitor, but the Bushwhackers have already been involved in some near fights, so we have a ref.

The ref warns Rich twice about flying elbows and pushing Dad from behind, but Dad tells him no sweat and plays through it. Dad doesn't have finesse, but he's in killer shape for a guy his age and even stronger than he looks. He plays smart, always stays between his man and the hoop, and picks up a lot of garbage rebounds.

Barbour is trash-talking me like Dennis Rodman, but I'm quietly working him over, bringing him out on me because my jumper is falling, then driving to the hoop when he leaves me room. It's illegal to dunk because the backboards can't handle it, so I'm setting them just over the rim. Barbour does have a nasty inside hook he lifts over me a couple of times, but I watch it close, and the third time he tries it, I slap it into the crowd, then land directly in front of him, staring.

When we have them down 19 to 17, they bring in Weeks, who is deadly from outside. At Hoopfest a regular basket counts as one and a normal three-pointer counts two. Dad waves Mott in, hands him the ball, and says, "End this shit." Weeks steps back and sinks a two-pointer for them, and we get the ball. I drive past Barbour to the hoop, flip the ball out to Mott, who pivots on his bionic leg to square up and sinks the long ball. Slammin' Mermen 21, Assholes 19.

Heidi jumps up and down, clapping with glee, with no sense of her father's humiliation. We try to shake their hands, but only Weeks and Neilson respond. Marshall slams the ball into the ground so hard it lands two courts away, and he and Barbour disappear into the crowd.

Dad waits until he's sure Rich is gone, then hoists Heidi onto his shoulders at her request. Chris dances around like he's been set free, Jackie claps his fins together like a baby seal, Simon thrusts a meaty fist into the air while Dan

210

runs over our stats to deaf ears. Tay-Roy and Kristen watch.

As we gather the last of our gear, we hear gasps on the other side of the court and look up to see the crowd part. I glimpse the muzzle of the deer rifle, think it's pointed at Dad, and scream his name, but Rich levels the barrel on Heidi, the one person whose loss would touch us all most. Dad whirls at the sound of my voice and instinctively dives directly into the path of the bullet. His body crashes to the pavement with a thud.

There is chaos. Later I will learn that Barbour followed Marshall back, trying to catch and stop him, and was actually the guy who got the gun away; and that Alicia threw herself over Heidi and the boys in an act that will go a long way toward getting her kids back in her care.

But in the moment, there is only me and Dad. He says, "Oh, man, this is bad."

I'm screaming for a doctor, but he puts his hand to my mouth. "Is Heidi okay?"

I spot her under Alicia, next to Georgia. "Yeah. She's okay. Hold on, Dad. They're getting help." All around me people holler for a doctor.

He shakes his head, and I see blood leaking onto the pavement. He says, "This doesn't feel good, T. J. I don't think we have much time."

"Dad, be *quiet*. Just relax. There's help."

"*Listen!*" He breathes slowly, and I hear air being sucked through the wound. "His name . . . was Tyler."

"What?"

"The little boy. Under the truck . . . I can see him. . . ." I hear the sucking sound again. "This isn't . . . the light and the tunnel thing. I just see him . . . remember. The widow . . . she was Stacy . . . Stacy Couples."

"Dad, hold on." His head is cradled in the crook of my arm, and I look up and scream again for help. The crowd moves in; there are sirens.

"I'm not going to make it, T. J." I can feel him giving up, relaxing. "Listen to me . . . I'm not afraid, but listen. Not one minute . . ." He starts to fade but fights back. "Not one minute . . . for revenge . . ."

"Dad, come on. Stay with me."

"Listen!"

I hold his head tighter.

"Not *one minute* for revenge. I've spent my life . . . looking back . . . wanting to change things. . . . This is okay. . . . Promise you won't . . ."

I glance over at Rich Marshall, pinned to the ground by Tay-Roy and Mike Barbour. Barbour is screaming at him. If I weren't with Dad, I'd kill him. "Dad . . ."

"Promise."

"Dad . . ."

"Promise!"

I do.

"You're going to . . . have to . . . forgive him, T. J. . . . He had no idea . . . what he was doing. . . ."

That was Jesus' last line. "Hold on, Dad."

"You're sure Heidi's okay?"

"She's okay, Dad. Alicia's got her."

He smiles faintly. "Guess I killed one and I saved one. Tell your mother . . ."

Oh, God, my mother.

"Tell her I love her."

"You'll tell her yourself, Dad. Just *hold* on."

"Tell her thanks."

He smiles, and I feel the most familiar feeling I know,

212

that of the deer slipping away. My father is gone. I didn't get a chance to tell him . . . he saved two.

There is a doctor, then paramedics. They pound his chest, give him mouth-to-mouth, hook him to the electronics, but Dad is gone. They don't pronounce him dead before placing him in the ambulance, but that's for my benefit. The cops cuff Rich, dragging him away; Chris Coughlin runs in circles, Mott stands silent on the edge of the court.

Whale Talk

The road between Cutter and New Meadows, Idaho, is mostly two-lane. Once you get through Spokane and cut south, the traffic is light during the middle of the week, though it's the only direct route between eastern Washington and southern Idaho. On a BMW cycle, staying within five or ten miles per hour of the speed limit, it's about a six-and-a-half-hour trip.

I pull into town from the north, pass the Pine Knot, which, from the outside, looks a lot like my father described it. At the intersection I turn right and cruise slowly down Main Street, taking in the town of just more than seven hundred people, stretching my imagination back thirty years. It's not much of a stretch. I see a sign for the cemetery and follow it, pulling the bike over at the gate. I place my helmet carefully on the backseat and walk in, reading the tombstones, looking for the little boy who changed my father's life.

It's a simple marker, laid flat in the ground. TYLER COU-PLES, next to his dates. He wasn't quite two. I kneel and run my hand over the ridges of the letters, checking the markers on either side for Stacy. She's not there.

In the Pine Knot I order a piece of pie and water. It's early afternoon on a Wednesday, and the place is empty but for the waiter, who is also the cook, who is also, it turns out, the owner.

He places the pie in front of me. "You're not from around here."

"Cutter. Up in Washington."

"What brings you down here?"

"Graduated from high school last spring," I say. "Taking a little bike trip."

"You're taking a bike trip to New Meadows, Idaho?"

I smile. "Listen, does a woman named Stacy Couples live around here? She'd be close to fifty."

"Stacy moved about eleven years ago," he says. "Right after her son Kyle graduated. Went to Boise."

A son. Jesus, that fits with the time my dad and Stacy— "She has a son?"

"Sure does."

"Do you know where he lives?"

The man points toward the back of the cafe. "He lives a half block that way. But he's buying the grocery store, and he runs some boats down the Salmon over in Riggins. Quite the entrepreneur, that Kyle."

"I'd like to meet him. We might know some people in common."

"Well, you can find him over at the store about twelve hours a day when he's not running the river. Bet he's there now."

The store is clean and quiet; a checker reads a Stephen King book behind the counter. She glances up to greet me when I walk in and points me toward the produce section when I ask for the owner.

"Kyle Couples?"

"The one and only. What can I do for you?" He's a big

man, dark and fit, somewhere in his late twenties or early thirties.

"I think we may have the same father."

He looks at me with surprise. "Excuse me?"

My ethnicity hasn't occurred to me. "Not biological," I say. "I'm adopted."

When he's past the shock, and I have a chance to tell him how I think we're related, Kyle invites me to his upstairs office. The walls are decorated with pictures of him on different motorcycles, most of them Harleys, all of them classic. Behind his cluttered desk is a blown-up photo of a huge gray whale diving.

"You like bikes," I say.

"I love bikes," he says back.

"And whales."

He smiles sheepishly. "Always had a thing for 'em. Don't know why. The year I graduated from high school, I took a bike trip to the coast, just south and west of Seattle. Went on a boat tour, got close enough for me to get that shot. I don't know. Just something about 'em. They have a kind of . . . majesty."

I stare at the picture. How in the world . . . ? They didn't know each other a day, and yet. . . . "Your mom lives in Boise?"

He looks away. "How'd you know that?"

"The guy at the Pine Knot. You talk to her much?"

"I don't talk to her at all," he says.

I back off, give him time to tell me.

"She just never really accepted me," he says finally. "I mean, hell, who could blame her? First time with a man after her husband is killed, and it ends in her kid getting killed and all kinds of shame for getting pregnant. I've heard stories about my mother, about how cool she was before I was born, before she lost her husband, before your dad . . . before Tyler got killed. But that wasn't the mom I ever knew. She was just absent. My aunt and uncle raised me, really. I lived with Mom and all, but by the time I was in second grade, I spent as little time there as I could."

"Man, I'm sorry."

"Not your fault," he says, and hesitates. "So my dad, what's he do?"

"Not much of anything now," I say. I haven't talked about that day with anyone but my mother and Georgia, but it's what I came here for. I tell him about Hoopfest, the events leading up to it.

"Jesus, that was my dad? We read about that."

"That was your dad." I tell him as much as I can about the effect killing Kyle's older brother had on him.

"Boy, nobody came out of that one, did they?"

"Maybe you and me," I say, and tell him about whale talk, how if we knew more about humans maybe we could accommodate one another better. All the time I'm saying it, he stares at the picture of the giant tail with a soft smile on his face. I swear to God, put a beard and a few tattoos on him, and he'd look like Dad spit him out.

"You graduated this year, huh?"

"Yeah." I don't say how hollow that day was for me.

"Going to school?"

"I was accepted to U Dub, but my heart's not in it, you know? Think I'll wait a year. Sell off some of Dad's bikes."

"Spend much time on the river up there?"

"Yeah, we've got a boat. I ski some. Wake board."

"Ever do any whitewater rafting?"

I tell him no.

"I could use some help," he says. "I've got some good guys working for me over there, but it's hard to run this place and keep an eye on that business as much as I should. You look in good shape. We're in the middle of the season now. I could train you. Even if you decide to go to school, it's great summer work. You can make a bundle."

I tell him I'll think about it.

He puts a hand on my shoulder. "I'd like to get to know you. You could fill in some holes for me. There's an . . . an emptiness when you can't get to your dad."

It's a feeling I know. "How soon do you need to know?"

"Anytime in the next thirty years," he says. "I'll be doing it at least that long. Hey, man, it's a rush."

"I'll get back to you one way or the other," I say. "And I'll be back."

I pick up my pack, stop at the door. "You'd have been proud of him," I say. "If he'd known about you . . . God, he'd have been down here in a minute."

I take the ride back to Cutter slow. Rich Marshall is in jail for the rest of his life, no possibility of parole. His attorney tried to plead down from first-degree murder because Rich actually killed someone different from the one he was aiming at. That may have saved him from the death penalty, but the prosecution successfully argued that he was going to kill *somebody,* and that was the premeditated part.

I didn't go to the trial. To tell the truth, I really didn't care how it turned out. I don't know what's the matter with me, but they could have let him off and I don't think I'd have felt a thing. All I know is my dad is dead. And that's all I care about.

Maybe I'm still numb, but maybe Dad passed something on to me in those few minutes he lay bleeding on the court. Maybe I heard him differently than I'd heard him before. Maybe what he said translated well into whale talk. *Not one minute for revenge.* He didn't want me living a life of what might have been. That was his life, and he wanted it stopped there. There are worse things a guy could do with his life than honor the wishes of a good and dying man.

Some positive things have come of all this. Alicia and Heidi and Things One and Two are permanent at our place now, and I think Alicia has some sense of what it means to step up, even if she discovered it late. Mom invited Icko to build living quarters on the edge of our property, and he's going to be a kind of caretaker for the place and live there free. He and his son are player/coaches for the South Park Mermen this summer, a slow-pitch softball team that travels around eastern Washington and northern Idaho losing softball games with astonishing regularity. Tay-Roy and Mott have gone their ways, but the heart of the team is a ghost of a shortstop, the world's largest first baseman, and a right fielder in a Cutter letter jacket that he removes only when he feels faint from the heat. Dan Hole keeps their stats.

Mike Barbour approached me at the funeral and shook my hand. He said, "I didn't know, man. I didn't." He was popping out of his suit, looked horribly uncomfortable, tears welling in his red-rimmed eyes. "Part of this is mine," he said. "I ain't askin' you to forgive me. I just want you to know I know that." Little acts of heroism.

219

Tonight, after Alicia and the kids are in bed, Mom and I put the whale tape into the VCR, turn up the sound, and sit in the porch swing listening, staring at the carpet of stars.

"God, Mom," I say. "Sometimes there's just no place to put this."

"Well," she says, "if there's no place to put it, maybe we don't need to put it anywhere."